A STRANGER IN THE FAMILY

At the age of three, Kit Philipson was abducted. He grew up adored by his adopted parents but on his mother's death bed she told him her terrible secret along with details of his real mother.

Isla Novello is thrilled to have her long-lost son back but not all of the family are happy to welcome Kit back into the fold. They are all concerned about their inheritance and are reluctant for him to investigate his disappearance. Kit is determined to find out the truth and embarks on an epic journey that takes him back to the horrors of Nazi Germany.

A STRANGER IN
THE FAMILY

A STRANGER IN THE FAMILY

by

Robert Barnard

Magna Large Print Books
Long Preston, North Yorkshire,
BD23 4ND, England.

British Library Cataloguing in Publication Data.

Barnard, Robert
    A stranger in the family.

    A catalogue record of this book is
    available from the British Library

    ISBN   978-0-7505-3478-9

First published in Great Britain in 2010 by
Allison & Busby Ltd.

Copyright © 2010 by Robert Barnard

Cover illustration Allison & Busby

The moral right of the author has been asserted

Published in Large Print 2011 by arrangement with
Allison & Busby Ltd.

Magna Large Print is an imprint of Library Magna Books Ltd.

Printed and bound in Great Britain by
T.J. (International) Ltd., Cornwall, PL28 8RW

PROLOGUE

August, 1939

The two children sat almost motionless on their seats as the landscape through the train windows became flatter. They didn't look at the country they were passing through, perhaps feeling that was somehow dangerous or forbidden. Periodically the girl looked down on her young brother, straightening his clothes, once giving him a smile which was not returned.

When there were sounds of footsteps in the corridor the girl pricked up her ears, and the little boy looked anxiously up at her.

'It's all right,' said the girl, patting his leg. 'Our papers are all in order. The man who came from Daddy said they were.'

'Why couldn't Mummy come too?' the boy asked, his face crumpled up. 'It was horrible saying goodbye to her.'

'I know it was. She'll come as soon as she can get things settled,' the girl said carefully. Her words were something decided in advance, said by rote.

'He's coming!' said one of the older boys in the carriage as footsteps were heard from the next compartment.

The door opened and a cheery face with a long nose and ruddy cheeks put his face round the door.

'What have we here? Eight children with eight tickets and eight sets of papers. How did I guess? Never mind. Now, I'll never remember your names...'

'I'm Hilde Greenspan and this is my brother Jürgen,' said the girl.

'Is that so? Very nice names too. But I think I'll do without names for the rest of you. Your papers were seen at Munich or Frankfurt when you boarded the train, were they not? So no need to– Wait a moment: we're stopping.'

He must have caught the look of panic on the girl's face because as he retreated to the corridor he turned back.

'Don't worry. This happens practically every trip. Routine. I just have to go and say my piece and then we'll be on our way.'

They heard his footsteps going to the end of the corridor and a window opening, talk beginning. Jürgen looked at his sister pleadingly.

'It's all right, little brother. The man smiled at us. Only good people smile at us these days.'

Minutes later the talk stopped and the window was pulled up. No footsteps were heard. Hilde's face showed that the tension was almost unbearable. Then the train started and slowly, slowly, it went through the station and out to a landscape of flat fields. Only then did the footsteps return. Hilde smiled a strained smile at her brother.

'Right. That didn't take long did it?' said the ticket collector.

'Why is your voice funny?' asked the boy called Jürgen.

'It doesn't sound funny, I just say sometimes words that you're not expecting. You see, I don't talk German. I talk Dutch.'

'What's Dutch?'

'Well, well. How old are you, young man?'

'I'm three. And four months.'

'Then you should know that the country next to Germany when you go north is called Holland or else the Netherlands, and the people there are Dutchmen. It's a bit complicated, isn't it? You only have one word for your country and its people and somehow we seem to have three. That's the last time I say anything good about Germany. But our two languages are very similar and one day we'll be friends, with God's help. Anyway, the thing to remember, the important thing, is that now we're in Dutch territory. Holland.'

The compartment suddenly changed in character. The children, of all ages from three to fifteen, looked at each other, smiled, mouthed a brief prayer, and shuffled

11

in their seats as if before they had been statues, but now had come to life.

'Thank you so much,' said Hilde.

'Nothing to thank me for. Now, Miss Hilde Greenspan, take a good look at my funny face. You might need a bit of help when you get to Waterloo. Try to keep me in view, and if you do need something or want to know something, come and ask me. Right? No need for papers now, but you'll need them on the boat.' He started out of the compartment. Then he turned back again.

'Good luck,' he said.

The children looked at each other.

'What a nice man,' said Hilde. The other children, especially Jürgen, nodded vigorously.

'I haven't had a stranger be so nice to me for years,' said a boy in his teens.

Later, when their papers had been examined and all had been found in order, Hilde and Jürgen stood on the prow of the ferry taking them away and tried to make their eyes penetrate the sea mist.

'When are we going home, Hilde?' asked Jürgen.

'I think that's where we are going,' said Hilde. She strained her eyes still further, as if that would enable her to see the future.

CHAPTER ONE

The Homecoming

2009.

The tall, skinny young man stopped outside the gate of number 35, which he had been aiming for since he came into Seldon Road. By doing a spot of mental arithmetic he had counted the detached and semi-detached houses and fixed on the dark-green painted house, a tacked-onto, half-timbered building from the Thirties.

He stopped and looked at the front garden. Now he knew he had come to the right place – knew from some memory, or the memory of a picture perhaps. In the centre of the small plot – the real garden was out the back he somehow knew – stood seven or eight rose bushes, in their winter bareness, and around them was a narrow, neat path of lawn, while bordering the road was a well-clipped hedge.

Very well cared for. A tidy, garden-proud person lived here. One first, new piece of knowledge. Perhaps he remembered it because the house owner was disinclined to change anything. Too busy? Or perhaps just hopeful that...

He shook himself back into consciousness of his situation. He had been here several minutes. He looked around. He caught no one looking at him, but one of the curtains had moved. An old neighbour, perhaps, who remembered when it had happened. Or was that dark event of the past part of the folk memory of the neighbourhood, passed on from the old to each new resident?

He put his hand down and clicked the latch of the gate. It was only a few steps to the front door. He couldn't say he remembered it, but when he looked down at the bottom panel it said something to him. He mustn't arouse comment or suspicion by standing there for too long. He rang the bell, which sounded soullessly and electronically through the house.

No footsteps came.

He looked at the lock. An old-fashioned one, a sturdy-key job. He resisted the inclination to look round again to see if he was watched. That could have someone ringing the police. He tried the handle of the door. It swung open, as if of its own accord, inviting him in. He crossed the threshold.

The beanpole boy shut the door carefully, as if in a dream. He looked around him. The hall was fairly newly decorated, he guessed. A rather indeterminate blue, as if a strong colour would have been too adventurous, a pastel one too old-fashioned. He thought that the woman of the house – that was how he had begun to think of her – was chivvied into having the hall done when it was far gone into shabbiness or decay, but had not put her heart into it.

He passed into the living room. The television was new: one of those widescreen jobs, just like his mother had had. The rug in front of the fireplace was also new – indefinite flowers against unidentifiable leaves. He looked up at the pictures. Photos of present-day young children in colour – children laughing at the photographer, children playing on a sunny beach. A reproduction of a Landseer sheepdog, and an urban landscape by night, with a woman walking beside a wall. They said little to him.

Of course, he didn't recognise them. A boy of three, as he had been, would have to bend backwards to see them, or lie on the floor, and then they would probably be too distant.

He passed back into the hall, then through to the kitchen. He was hit by an overwhelming smell. Two smells. He recognised one of them – it was caramelised sugar. Toffee. The other was of a cake – some kind of curranty bun.

He was so rapt in the past that he jumped when the handle of the kitchen door was

15

pulled down. Through the frosted glass he could only see a shape, but he thought it was a woman's, and was glad.

'What are you doing in my kitchen?'

There was only a slight quaver in the voice. He said the first thing that came into his head.

'I thought you wouldn't mind.'

She looked at him and he looked at her. He would have guessed she was about sixty, but he knew she was several years younger. Her grey hair was pinned back, her face was lined with plenteous wrinkles, her mouth was set as if in a stern, unforgiving line, perhaps to conquer misfortune.

'You're not–?'

'I'm Kit now. Christopher.'

'But before?'

'I was Peter before.'

The colour drained from her face. 'You're alive!'

It was as if they were thinking of what they should do. The young man's bewilderment was natural and total, but the woman took some time before she did the right thing, the inevitable thing.

'Come here,' she said. And she took him in her arms, he letting out little sobs of pleasure and relief, and she following suit. She only came up to his chest, and when she pushed him away she gave a little laugh.

'It was a lot easier to hold you when you were a baby!'

He laughed too, and wiped his eyes.

'I remember your hugs, or I think I do... It's difficult to say, but I do remember when I had my new ... my new mother,' he said firmly, as if he had taken a resolution, 'when she hugged me she had make-up on, and at first I didn't like the smell and took a long time getting used to it.'

'I never did go in much for make-up.'

'Eventually I came quite to like it, but I soon got to the age when you don't like being hugged by your mother, not when there are other people around.'

The woman's face showed conflicting emotions – jealousy that another woman had enjoyed his childish hugs, pleasure that he had compared those hugs unfavourably with hers, controlled rage that she had been denied all the pleasures of seeing this one of her children grow up.

'You remembered the hugs, then?'

'I do now. I suppose I'd forgotten them for a long time. Some memories have been coming back to me in the last few weeks since I learnt who I was. I remembered mostly your legs.'

'My legs?'

'Because I was down at their level. You wore sandals all the time – at least during the summer, I suppose.'

'During that last summer, before...' She couldn't say it. 'It was such a hot one,' she lamely concluded.

'I remember Dad's legs too, with the slippers on his feet. He never put them on properly, and trod the backs down with his heels.'

'You remember quite a lot,' she said shyly.

'Yes. Or maybe I'd just put the images at the back of my mind, and they were waiting for me ... waiting for now, I suppose.'

'Yes. For now.'

'Is my bedroom the same as it used to be?'

'You remember it, then?'

'Yes.' He stood with his hands nursing his chin. 'The walls were green, with cut-out pictures pasted on them. I don't remember what they were, but I think Donald Duck was one. And when I saw *Pinocchio* on television once I recognised the nose. And there was a little rocking chair... Or was that in my other home?'

She walked into the hall, then turned and put out her hand. He came to her and put his hand in hers. It was like being taken to a secret garden, or into a magic wardrobe. Neither said anything, and when they came to the landing his mother dropped his hand and let him choose the door to go through. He did it without hesitation. It was like passing an exam, but a pleasant one. The room hit him hard: it was as if it had been preserved in aspic. The green walls were exactly as when he had last seen them, and so were the pictures pasted on. Now he recognised Noddy, and the seven dwarfs – and there was Donald Duck and Pinocchio. He turned and looked at his mother, he smiling shyly, she with new, sparkling eyes.

'There's the rocking chair,' she said, with a break in her voice.

He walked over and rocked it, and then he found his mother suddenly in his arms again, sobbing and laughing.

'You've come home,' she said. And he said, perhaps too quickly: 'Yes, I've come home.'

He had known this was what his mother would feel, but he knew it would be some time before he could really share the emotion. Now he had acknowledged it rather than felt it. A stiffening of her body suggested she was acknowledging that too.

'It's just as I saw it last time,' he murmured.

'I kept it like that, specially.'

'The last time must have been when we went to ... where was it?'

'Trepalu. It was at Trepalu it happened.'

'That's Sicily, isn't it?

'Yes. I had to force myself to go back once. It was hideous. The memories were so bitter.'

The boy nodded, then resumed his

scrutiny of the room.

'It's like my childhood is here,' he said. 'My early childhood.'

'Yes. You weren't allowed much of one,' said his mother. Kit, or Peter, looked at her uncomprehending, then shook his head.

'Oh, I had a childhood after the one here,' he said. 'A happy one too. Only it was very different.'

'Yes, I see,' said his mother, vowing to be more careful.

'You've got to understand that my new mother and father were good to me. They saw me as a late gift.' The woman obviously suppressed a tart comment, perhaps that Kit had been in the nature of a purchase rather than a gift to his second pair of parents. 'I'm going to have to think what to call you,' the young man said. '"Mother" I don't much care for. I've always used it for the mother who raised me, so it would be confusing. I'm not keen on "Ma" or "Mum", though they're less confusing. What is your Christian name?'

'Isla. It's a Scottish name, you know.'

'Oh, I know. I come from Scotland, remember.'

She looked at him, astonished.

'But I can't remember! I never knew.' Kit shook his head in self-reproach.

'Of course you didn't know. But somehow I thought that you did... I was brought up in

20

Glasgow, and I'm going to university at St Andrews now. Perhaps I thought that my accent would give me away.'

'It's very slight. Isla is really a river. It's odd, isn't it? Like calling a boy "Thames" or "Tyne". We're going to have to find out about each other, aren't we? Come downstairs again. We'll have something to eat.'

'I'd like that. Something light.'

When they got down Isla took him into the dining room, the smaller of the two downstairs rooms, with a sturdy table, and photographs again.

'What would you like? Scrambled eggs? Pasta and cheese? An omelette?'

'Macaroni cheese sounds good. I can't manage spaghetti.'

'Use a spoon in your left hand,' said his mother promptly, 'and wind up a forkful against it. The Italians don't need a spoon but they're born to it and we're not. Not yet anyway.'

Left to himself Kit looked around him. The room was not unlike the living room but less used, less lived in. There were photographs on the bookcase, and in the middle of the table. Kit guessed his mother never used the room when she was on her own. One of the snaps showed a couple of about thirty, another a smart-looking woman in her late twenties, then there were several of children, a fair girl and a dark boy.

None of him.

Until, going to the window to look out, he found one on the window ledge, almost hidden by the curtains. He felt sure it was him. There were some of him at an early age in the photo album at home in Scotland, and they were very similar. Here his childish image looked out at the photographer from a beach (Trepalu?) with a complete confidence and love. He wondered how long it had been before he had felt the same confidence in his new family, the Philipsons.

But it was natural to assume there had been problems of adjustment. No child could experience a complete change of parentage and retain the same confidence that he'd had before. And it was natural, too, that Isla should keep any photograph she had of him in an inconspicuous place. To catch sight of it, to be reminded of her loss, would be to have a daily dose of pain.

The telephone rang and he hastily put the photograph down, as if he didn't want to be caught looking at it. But the phone was in the hall, and he heard Isla say: 'Oh, Micky – I was hoping you'd ring... But you'll have to make time, Micky... Just ten minutes, I don't need any more. I've got something for you here... Why should I need a reason for getting a surprise for you? Anyway it's Becky's birthday soon... Well, three days, three weeks, what does it matter? You can't collect it, but you must come and inspect it... All right, ten minutes will do. I'll see you at a quarter to two.'

Kit heard her bustle back to the kitchen, and then there wafted into the dining room a warmth and a smell that had cheese and Italy combined, and made the house suddenly seem home-like.

'We'll eat before Micky comes,' his mother said, bustling back. 'He's not interested in food. I say he'd never eat at all if his wife didn't force it down him. He wouldn't thank me for saving any for him.'

'It smells glorious.'

She gestured him to a chair, and began filling two large pasta dishes.

'I hope you don't mind me calling you "it" to Micky; I want you to be a total surprise. He'll be expecting a big parcel with pink bows on it for Becky. That's his daughter, the only girl – she's a real love – more charm than she knows what to do with.'

'And Micky is–'

'Oh Lord! You don't remember? I am sorry. Micky is your elder brother. He was seven when you were born. We all spoilt you because you were a late arrival – un-expected, like.'

'I think you'd better tell me what family I've got,' said Kit, suddenly nervous. His mother paused in her eating, blaming herself for neglecting such an obvious duty.

23

'Two brothers. Micky is twenty-nine, Dan is nineteen. One sister, Maria, is thirty. They all live here in the Leeds area. Dan is in Australia at the moment – seems to be enjoying it, so we won't be seeing him for a while. Micky lives in Pudsey. I've had to help him a bit: he started a family early, got married in a bit of a hurry. Maria lives in Ilkley, married to a man well older than herself, but they're very happy and have a lovely house.'

Kit suspected a submerged disapproval of her daughter, for marrying age in order to get money.

'What about my dad?' he asked.

'Oh, he's very sick. Won't last long. He's in a home.'

There were several questions to be asked, but Kit took a lightning decision not to ask them. Her answer had been brusque.

'Well, that brings me up to date,' he said.

'And it's time to tell me about you. Then I won't make any embarrassing mistakes. Why not start with your name?'

'My name is Kit or Christopher Philipson. I'm an only child – you could have guessed that, I suppose: that must have been the reason for ... you know.'

'Yes.' The monosyllable showed an element of steel had entered the voice.

Anyway, my parents were Genevieve and Jürgen. My mother was a part-time teacher in the Glasgow University Fine Arts Department. She'd been a full lecturer before I ... came along. She went back to part-time work when I'd got settled. She never put it like that to me. She'd have said "old enough". She always spoke as if I'd been born to her.'

His mother's lips were pursed.

'But surely she must have had a story ready for friends and neighbours? They would have known she hadn't been pregnant.'

'Eventually – not long before she died – she told me I'd been adopted. I expect she'd told them the same. The simpler the better, and the more likely to be accepted without comment.'

'I suppose so. What about your d– your other dad? What did he do?'

'He was a journalist – rather a high-up one. Worked in the offices of one of the Glasgow dailies, and ended up deputy editor. Very nicely off – the house was plenty big enough for us three and the au pair of the moment.'

'Oh ... there was an au pair?'

He ignored undercurrents.

'Yes, right up to my mother's death. The au pair was really just a foreign maid by then.' He cast her a sharp look. 'They never foisted me off on her. She was just someone around when they were not.'

'Oh yes, I'm sure. They wouldn't have foisted you off when they presumably had … wanted you so much.'

'That's right. I really did always feel wanted. Anyway, there was a grandmother early on – my mother's mother – she died when I was about seven or eight. My father's birth father was sometimes mentioned, but it was never suggested that we went to see him or he should come and stay with us. I suspect he must have lived abroad.'

'Why do you think that?'

'He – my father – came to Britain in one of those trains from Germany.'

'The Kindertransport?'

'That's right. That was in 1939, and he was not much more than a baby, brought by his sister, my aunt Hilda. He was three.'

'Your age.'

'Yes … Jürgen and Hilda were taken in by the Philipsons in Hampstead, stayed with them after the war, and took their name. I remember the Philipson grandparents a little, but by then they were very old. Jürgen's real father was Austrian or German, I forget which. He got out of Vienna during the war but I don't know any more about him, and nothing about his wife, my grandmother.'

'I see… Can't you eat any more?'

Kit pushed his pasta away and smiled.

'I'm afraid I'm too excited. It was lovely.'

26

'Well, we'll clear the plates away, and I'll put coffee on... Oh, there's Micky now. Don't get up. I don't want him to see you through the window. You stand out.'

She hurried back to the kitchen. Kit stood up when he heard the front door open, as if he wanted to use his height to counter any elder-brother assertions by Micky. I must be Peter now, he said to himself. As he was saying it, the door was opened and a plump young man – fleshy anyway, in spite of his proclaimed lack of relish for eating – was ushered in. His face was artless, and he was dressed in white overalls with traces of several colours of paint. He turned round, back to the door.

'You didn't tell me you had a visitor, Mum.' He turned back to Kit and held out his hand. 'I'm Micky Novello. I won't interrupt, I'm just in and out.' But his voice faded on the last word. 'But you ... you remind me of–'

'I'm Kit Philipson. Who do I remind you of?'

'I don't know... You, Mum, I think.' He turned around again, but she took hold of his shoulders and pushed him towards Kit.

'It's Peter, you great idiot. Your little brother Peter. All grown up.' And she went back towards the kitchen and left them alone with their past.

'I used to be Peter Novello,' said Kit

quietly. There was a moment's silence, then Micky sat down on one of the dining chairs.

'God Almighty,' said Micky; 'Where did you come from, then?'

'Glasgow, actually. Where I grew up.'

'We always thought you must be in Sicily or Corsica, or somewhere dangerous and glamorous like that. Where the people clam up and keep outsiders away.' He suddenly got up and threw his arms around Kit's shoulders, which he could just reach. 'Welcome home, boy.' He sat down again with a thump. 'But who did you grow up with?'

'The Philipsons – Jürgen and Genevieve. The people I thought till a while ago were my birth parents.'

'Bloody 'ell,' said Micky, wiping his eyes. 'This is an experience. Like a dream.'

'It's the same for me. Except that I had no idea what was coming. I hope it's a pleasant dream for you.'

'Oh, it is, boy, it is.'

'Can I ask you a question?'

'Yeah – go on.'

'I gather Dad – my Leeds dad – is in some kind of home.'

'That's right, he is.'

'Is he senile? Alzheimer's, is it? If it is, is that why he's not here, being nursed by Mum? It must be very severe.'

'It's not that severe, and he's not dangerous. That's not the reason. Mum obviously hasn't told you that he and she separated two years after you were ... abducted. They have hardly had anything to do with each other in the last seventeen years. He's in a nursing home, but it's not a bad one. Mostly when I go to see him he makes perfect sense.'

'You see him?'

'Now and then. We've always got on OK, Dad and me.'

'What does Isla think about that?'

'I've never asked her. I don't even know if she knows, though she could easily guess. We never talk about Dad.'

'I told your mother the only memory I have of him is his feet – stuffed into his slippers with the backs down and the heels exposed.'

'That's my dad. Still is.'

'I don't have any other memories, good or bad.'

'They shouldn't be bad, but they would very likely be patchy. The worst you could say is that he was so busy he didn't have much time for any of us. I remember his playing very little part in our lives till we were old enough to play cricket and kick a ball round.'

'My... other dad wasn't much into sport. Perhaps it was one of the English things that never really gelled with him. But he liked sleeping through a cricket match.'

'Wasn't he English? Was he Italian?

'German Jewish. Got out just in time. Always felt relief and gratitude to the British, but also a bit of guilt.'

'I suppose he would. Will you be stopping here with us?'

'For a few days. I'm in a hotel – a nice, inconspicuous one on the road to Kirkstall Abbey. I won't stay long this time. There's still a lot to be done after my mother's death.'

'Was that recent?'

'About six weeks ago. She left everything very orderly – she was that kind of person – but there still seems a lot for me to see to.'

'I wonder if you'll come round to my place? See the family, like. My wife is called Pat, and we've got three, just like Mum and Dad. Ben, Becky and Tom.'

Kit could not hold himself back from saying: 'Your mum and dad had four, Micky. Four.'

'Sorry! I'm really sorry.' And he did look shamefaced. 'It's just that after a bit we didn't talk about you a lot. And the reason was Mum – it upset her. She'd go quiet, wipe a tear – you know how it is with women. So it meant that you were ... not forgotten, but only there in the background. I had memories of you but over the years they have mostly faded.'

'I understand. I'd love to come and meet you and your family.'

Micky said: 'Tell Mum I've got to go back to work,' and slipped out the front door. When his mother came back the talk started – not structured: a mixture of gossip, impressions, exam results and future ambitions. Isla learnt that her long-lost son had done well in A levels and had started at St Andrews University two Septembers ago. He and his adoptive mother had both thought it better that he didn't go to the university she worked for. They talked about food they liked – Italian in Kit's case, Isla liking the old English dishes as well. Kit and Isla both drank wine, both disliked English beer, and Kit regretted that there were no Yiddish meals or drinks that his father – sorry! my Glasgow father – had liked which he could have tried, because he'd heard Yiddish cuisine was fabulous. And so it went on.

Isla tried to persuade him to stay the night, but Kit thought that was too much in one day: he would prefer to be on his own now, so he could sit back and think about the whole experience of reuniting with his family. Isla accepted this (she had to do something similar, after all) and went to ring the taxi firm they used.

'I suppose tomorrow I'd better go to the police,' said Kit, as they waited at the front door.

'Police?' said Isla, seeming to tense up. 'But why?'

'Well, I must still be on their books as a lost person. A lost child probably, though they won't be surprised I've grown up.'

'But the Leeds police had very little to do with the investigation. As we said, the abduction happened in Italy – Sicily in fact – and the Italian police were involved, of course, so the English police mostly left it to the Italians.'

'I see. But there was a bit of publicity in the English press, surely? I'd have thought the English police would have responded to that.'

'Very little that I remember. The Italians considered it their case. I expect the name had something to do with it.'

'The name?'

'Your name. Our name. Novello.'

Some enlightenment came into Kit's face.

'I just thought Novello was the name of some singer or other. I never thought of it as an Italian name.'

'This looks like your taxi,' said Isla.

She kissed him goodnight with emotions that Kit thought might be love, thankfulness, and, strangely, fear.

CHAPTER TWO

Party Time

The next day, in the evening, Isla took Kit round to Micky's, so that he could make the acquaintance of Micky's family. Isla insisted that it be an evening party, and that the children could 'stop up late for once, surely'. She was one of those grandparents, Kit noted with amusement, who courts the approval of the new generation. Early that morning she had rung her youngest son, Dan, in Australia, told him she had something special up her sleeve, and that she would ring him from Micky's that evening in what would be early morning time in Australia. Kit had intended that day to go along to the police headquarters in central Leeds, but he slept so little in the first part of the night, and so exhaustedly in the latter part of it, that he felt ragged when he woke up and postponed the visit. He wandered round the vicinity of his hotel, starting with Kirkstall Abbey, noticing little, but deep in thought. He had a pub lunch in Headingley, surrounded by students who, except in accent, seemed identical to the ones he was used to in St Andrews. Late in the afternoon he caught a bus for Isla's.

The party had been set for seven-thirty, and Isla insisted that they call a taxi. 'Make a bit of a splash,' she explained. Kit didn't see why they needed to – thought it was either so Isla could drink without having to think of driving home, or maybe that the splash would symbolise instant and total acceptance of his claim to be Peter Novello. He went along with her wishes, feeling that he wanted to know all there was to know about her, and that included her tastes and prejudices. When the cab got to the Pudsey home of his brother's family, the door opened while he was paying the driver, and a substantial young woman appeared – in her thirties, fleshy, with a low-cut blouse and a long green skirt on. His sister-in-law, Kit presumed. She had a smile as wide as a chat show hostess's. Big and bossy said Kit to himself. Well meaning maybe, but that made it worse if anything. He could see Micky being smothered in a marriage with such a woman.

'You're Kit – no prizes for guessing that. I'm Pat, Micky's wife. Micky said you were good-looking, and for once he's right. Micky, come and welcome your brother–'

'I've welcomed him back.'

'–to your home, I was going to say.' She caught Kit's eye straying to the windows of her house, where were grouped adults and children, gazing at him with the voracity usually inspired only by a national celebrity. The sight filled Kit with something between embarrassment and fear. 'Now come on in. You can't say "hello" to your family through a window frame. And your family is what we've got for you: all the available Novellos.'

She put her arm around him and led him through the hall to the sitting room. Kit was conscious that Micky and Isla were bringing up the rear and weren't saying anything – maybe in some kind of apprehension as to how he would be received. If so, there was no reason for it: Pat surged forward and carried all before her, as she probably always did.

'These are our three – Becky, Tom and Ben. Say "hello" to your new uncle, all of you. This is Wendy Maclean, Dan's partner. Dan is in Australia playing football, or soccer as they call it, and doing some job in insurance. This is your sister Maria. That's right – give her a kiss. It's a long time since you had a sister, I believe. Her husband is called Ivor – Ivor Battersby. He can't be here tonight because he's away on business – says he'll be here in spirit. And this is my Auntie Flora, who's here because we love having her, and she's a marvellous helper with the children.'

'Hello, Auntie Flora,' said Kit, feeling ridiculous.

'You'll have noticed that no one here has a drink, not even the children,' continued Pat. 'I wanted to wait until you arrived – you and Mum, of course. Because the party only begins now: you are the party, and I want you all to get yourselves drinks from the sideboard, and when you've got them, we'll all have a toast... What will you have, Kit?'

'A red wine, please.'

Kit was getting the idea that Pat was an organiser – not just of her own family, but of everyone and everything in sight. Things had to happen as she planned for them to happen. Poor old Micky, he thought. He had sensed that Isla was not enamoured of her daughter-in-law.

'Here we are,' said Pat, bustling back. 'A Spanish red. Now ... has everyone got a glass? You children? Yes, of course you have. Now, keep on your feet everyone for the toast... Right...! Everyone say it: "Welcome home, Kit."'

'Welcome, Kit.'

'Welcome back, Kit.'

'Welcome home, Kit.'

Everyone said something appropriate, and Kit broke the tie with Pat by going round from person to person to thank them for their welcome – and perhaps to pick out by their voices those who had welcomed him or welcomed him back, but had not welcomed him *home*. Was it significant that she'd toasted him as Kit rather than Peter?

He sat down on a battered leather sofa beside his sister Maria, sipping his drink as she rather suspiciously sipped hers.

'You know, I think I always knew I had a sister,' he said. 'I didn't have much in the way of memories, but that much I did know.'

'It's sweet of you to say so,' said Maria. 'I was eleven when you disappeared, and I worried for a long time that we'd fade from your memory.'

'No. Never entirely. And I remembered my room. I could almost describe everything in it to Isla yesterday.'

He saw Maria registering how he referred to his mother. Maria was a slim, almost elegant young woman, dressed older than she was, perhaps to minimise the age difference with her husband. The hair was done especially for this impromptu family party, and the face was welcoming, except perhaps for the small, narrow mouth, and the eyes which were sharp – even calculating.

'I'm glad you could describe your room. Over the years it's become almost a mausoleum, but we never protested because it was Mum's decision, and after all, when Micky and I had moved out there was no particular use for it.'

'I get the impression – correct me if I'm wrong – that since our parents separated Isla has been ... call it the head of the family.'

Maria nodded vigorously.

'Oh, she has. Pat may dispute that now and then, but Mum has been in charge ... naturally enough, I'd say. They were divorced, by the way, Dad and Mum. When you were with us they were Catholic, at least nominally.'

'I don't suppose I knew what that meant. I was so young.'

'No, I suppose you wouldn't. But after they'd separated Mum let all that slide, and we none of us today would say "Catholic" if we were asked our religion. Oh, except Dad, perhaps.'

'He still is?'

She shrugged.

'Search me. I haven't talked to him for years. And he went along with the divorce, so he'd have to be a very bad Catholic indeed, wouldn't he?'

'Micky says he's pretty au fait with things sometimes, at other times quite far gone.'

'I know,' she said, seizing on the point quickly. 'That's why I can't see any point in going to visit him. He lost interest in us anyway, even while he had all his marbles. He's lucky to have found somewhere that will look after him well.'

'The nursing home?'

'The Four Bells. Sounds like a pub, doesn't it? Micky says he's perfectly happy there. But Mum's the one you need to talk to. She's been head of the family for as long as I can remember. I think Dad couldn't stand all the fuss about the abduction. Your abduction – sorry, your being here takes some getting used to.'

'Of course it does.'

'So Dad just moved out, and moved on. In the early days we met him, went out with him now and then. But then it sort of stopped. We didn't want it and he didn't want it – that's how I read it now.'

'So if there was any problem, you went to your mum with it?'

'Our mum. Yes, we did. Oh, I don't mean she was one of those matriarchs. We may have taken problems to her, but in the end we did what we thought right, or best, or whatever. Like when I married.'

'Ah! Yes, I did get the feeling that–'

Maria shot a quick glance over her shoulder, and said: 'You must come round as soon as Ivor gets back from his trip. It was planned long ago, so there was no way he could come tonight. He'll be so excited to meet you.'

That embarrassed Kit.

'I don't feel exciting. I was just a kid who got abducted.'

He stood up. A look shot round the room assured him that the person seated with her back to Maria's position on the sofa was the one whom Pat had called Aunt Flora. He guessed that she might be a collector and disseminator of gossip. He let his gaze wander gracefully around as he poured himself a second glass of Rioja from the wine box. He felt he wanted to talk to someone who was not too obviously of the family, but rejected Aunt Flora as not someone whom a long-lost son would want to spend much time on. He wandered instead over to a niche by a window, where stood, with a lurid-coloured liquid in her hand, the girlfriend or partner of his brother Dan.

'Hello, you're Wendy, aren't you?'

'Yes, Wendy Maclean.'

She squeezed out words, as if they were rationed.

'And you're my brother Dan's girlfriend, aren't you? I'm glad they asked you.'

'Oh, they didn't. Dan rang me and told me to go along, so I rang Pat and told her I was coming.'

Kit gaped.

'Let me get this straight. We're going to ring Dan later to tell him I've suddenly turned up out of the blue, but in fact he already knows and has sent you along to report on my reappearance. Is that right?'

'No, not really. He doesn't know you've reappeared. He knows – from his mother – that the Novellos are meeting tonight, partying, and that he'll be rung up with some surprising news. He didn't say much to me on the phone – too mean to run up big phone bills. He'll be surprised by your return to the family fold but Isla's promise of a surprise may have taken the edge off his. You are the big surprise the Novello family have hoped for for twenty years. He was only a baby when you went out of his life, but he's lived with all the talk about you.'

Kit digested this.

'I see. And what will be his reaction, do you think?'

'Oh, it'll just be a question of money. It always is with Dan. He left the country because someone told him he could get a whopping wage from a first-rate Australian soccer team.'

'And has he found he can't?'

'He's found there's no such thing as a first-rate Australian soccer team.'

There seemed to be considerable glee in her voice.

'I see. I did wonder when I heard he had a second job over there in insurance. Perhaps he's selling it door to door. Soccer doesn't have that big a hold Down Under. And I still don't see what my return to the family has to do with money.'

'He'll be imagining that at best your mother's estate will be divided up into four not three equal portions. At worst, you – as

41

favourite and long-lost child – will cop the lot. That really would cheese him off.'

'The question of money and inheritances hasn't come up with my mother. That's how important it is. Besides, she's still young. I don't want a share of her estate. I was the only child of my ... my other family, and I inherited the whole estate. That's more than enough for me. Too much, if you want to know the truth. Because I don't like all the responsibility.'

'Worth a bundle were they, then, your other parents?'

'Not really. Just comfortably off.'

Calculation flooded into her lightly mascaraed eyes.

'Depends what you mean by "comfort-ably". I find I can always use a little extra. No – quite a lot extra, if you want to know the truth.'

'Sounds like my money-conscious brother has made the wrong choice if he wants to hold on to his ill-gotten gains,' said Kit. Wendy put out her tongue, but undressed him with her eyes. 'Anyway, we can only talk about an "estate" because the price of pretty ordinary houses has gone up like crazy, though they've plummeted since the crunch. Isla's fairly ordinary house, divided by three or four, won't amount to riches by a long chalk. Dan had better stick to scoring goals for the best team he can find in

Australia. Better still, come home and play for a Premier League team.'

Wendy began caressing his hair, forming the lock that fell over his eye around her finger in a parody of a ring.

'He's not that good. You're cute – you know that?'

'Oh, I know it,' said Kit, getting up. 'I've been told it by half the nubile girls in Glasgow.'

'Well, they're right. Don't go–'

'I've got to meet all the family before I talk to your money-mad boyfriend.'

But in fact he landed up with the family member he already knew. Micky was standing by a bookcase that mostly contained recipe books. He was surveying the gathering with a satisfied but slightly cynical eye.

'You did well to get away,' he said, as Kit came near. 'She's a one-woman disaster zone. I'm afraid our brother Dan always chooses girls who are like-minded to himself.'

'Not a good idea?' said Kit, knowing the answer.

'The worst possible idea. Dan could only be saved by a sweet and sensible little thing who wanted a cosy nest and three or four children to look after.'

'Instead of which, all he and Wendy share is an obsession about money.'

'Exactly. Standing here I could almost see

the realisation crossing Wendy's face that Dan was never going to make the big bucks, and that you were a better bet.'

'In her dreams. By the way, she seems to think that Dan will feel rather threatened by my reappearance.'

'I suppose he may be,' said Micky, thinking. 'He'll be totting up the financial implications.'

'That's what darling Wendy thought. Not that Isla is likely to die for many years, but how much of an "estate" will there be? Say that the house in Seldon Road would have fetched fifty thousand fifteen years ago, and now could fetch two hundred thousand. A very nice increase in value, but is two hundred thousand that big a deal, however it's divided up?'

'To people with nothing much it's a nice little sum. And Dan and I have nothing much. You're forgetting–'

But Kit, who was preternaturally alert at this gathering of the clan, had noticed the little line of Micky's children, standing by the door, their eyes fixed unalterably on him.

'Your brood?' he asked Micky. 'Becky and Ben and something else?'

'Tom.'

'Why are they looking at me like that?'

'Because you've always been just a name to them all their lives, someone they've always assumed was long dead – as frankly we've all made a similar deduction, even though we all hoped you were alive. And then suddenly you turn up, alive – large as life, in fact. You ought to be some kind of ghost, but you look perfectly normal – ordinary, if you don't mind the word.'

'I don't. Call them over. They can poke me and find out that I'm like everyone else, then perhaps they can forget about me, or at least let me alone.'

'Becky! Tom! Ben! Come and meet your new uncle.'

They walked over eagerly, their eyes glued to his face, Becky put out her hand.

'Hello, Uncle Kit.'

The rest followed her lead, as they seemed to do in most things: 'Hello, Uncle Kit.'

'We thought you'd prefer to be called Kit,' said Becky.

'I do. I forgot the "Peter" quite quickly, when I was a very little boy. Now, what do you want to ask me, Becky?'

She had it off pat.

'What did it feel like to be abducted? What did they do to you?'

'Nothing very much,' said Kit, feeling a wave of disappointment run through the children. 'The people who took me just told me that my mother was very ill, and they were going to find me another mummy who would take care of me while the one I knew was ill.'

45

'That wasn't true, was it?'

'No, it wasn't.'

'I suppose they demanded a ransom for you, didn't they?'

Kit looked genuinely surprised.

'Do you know, I'm not sure. Your grandma would know better than I do. I never heard that they did, but my mother – my new mother – was very ill when she told me about how I had come to her, so I couldn't really ask her questions.'

'Well, they usually do, the people who nap kids. Pirates and that.'

'Perhaps,' said Micky, 'your grandma called it an abduction, not a kidnapping, for that reason – there was never a ransom demand. I certainly never heard of one, and I was about ten at the time, and knew all about kidnapping. Maybe the kidnappers got money from your second family, the ones you'd been abducted for.'

Kit shrugged.

'I don't know. I'd be surprised if there was any arrangement of that sort. And if so my other mother wouldn't have told me. It would have made it sound too much as if they'd bought me.'

'Well, they did, didn't they?' said Becky brutally. 'Did you like your other mummy?'

'Yes, I did. I loved her.'

This caused Becky in particular to think furiously.

'If I'd been ab ... ducted,' she said finally and cautiously, 'I don't think I'd have loved the man who called himself Daddy but who wasn't really my daddy.'

The caution was glaring, and proved her to be a truth-loving child.

'Go along with you,' said Micky, shooing them with his hand. 'You've had your time in the spotlight with Kit, now go and have some fun.'

'There's never any fun at adult parties,' protested Becky. But she marshalled the other two to go into the dining room, where the food was laid out.

'I interrupted you,' said Kit to Micky. 'You were about to say something.'

'Was I?' said Micky. 'I forget.'

'Something about Isla's money.'

'Oh... Oh yes.' Micky had clearly not forgotten, but had had an access of caution since beginning the subject. 'Well...' he looked around, taking in the figure of Auntie Flora, now in a nearby armchair, 'maybe now is not the time. Let's just say Mum doesn't struggle along on the standard old-age pension. There's more.'

'Could you manage a lunchtime drink?' asked Kit. 'Not tomorrow – I'm hoping to go to the police. Say Thursday?'

'That would be fine. The Vesper Gate in Kirkstall – I'm working there that day. What are you going to the police for?'

47

'To try to find out what, if anything, their investigations produced back in 1989, when the abduction happened.'

'But surely all the investigation was done by the Sicilian police?'

'Maybe – if they were not bought off by the Mafia or the Camorra, or just couldn't be bothered. But you're forgetting there must have been a British dimension.'

'Why?'

'Because I landed up with a new family in Glasgow.'

Micky looked troubled but then shook himself and murmured: 'You're right.'

'Though of course, the British police didn't know that at the time,' said Kit. 'And presumably still don't know.'

'Yes. Of course ... that's true. Most of the investigation at the time was into the Mediterranean countries. The Sicilian police thought you would be pretty conspicuous, with your light-brown hair and English features.'

'Right,' said Kit. 'How did you know that?'

'It's something Mum always mentioned when your disappearance came up... Oh look – we're going in for the nosh-up.'

The guests were trooping across the hall to the dining room, where the large table was crowded with plates – quiches, pork pie, plates of meat and fish, salads and sandwiches, with wine boxes on side tables and plenty of coke and orange pop for the children. As Kit queued and selected he found to his annoyance that he was next to Aunt Flora but way away from any of the other guests. He expected the worst when she pulled at the sleeve of his jacket. The face that looked up at his was avid to impart knowledge.

'Do you know how your family got their money?'

It wasn't the sort of question one got asked every day. Kit turned away to indicate his indifference to money.

'I believe my birth father was partner in a solicitor's firm.'

'That wasn't where the money came from.'

'I really don't–'

'The money came from ice cream.'

'Eh...? I mean, I beg your pardon?'

'Ice cream. The Italian firms that cornered the market in Scotland.'

'Oh, I've heard all about that.'

'Of course you have. Everybody has. You being Scottish by adoption too. That's what Pat told me. It's notorious, is all that. It was bribes from both sides – the old game. Doesn't do to be sniffy about your birth when you've got that in the background, does it?'

'I can't imagine Isla being sniffy about anything.'

'Oh, you've got a lot to learn. I suppose

49

you know your mother's never been the same since you were abducted?'

'I can understand that. Did you know her back then?'

'Oh no. I mean it's what everybody says.'

'Well, let's hope that the everybody who says it has known her better and longer than you have.'

'Oh, snooty!' said Aunt Flora, with a satirical twist to her face. Kit put his plate forward, spooned up prawns on to it, and went back to the sitting room.

'You've made a wonderful spread,' he said, sitting down next to Pat.

'Thank you. Not bad for short notice. The only way we can get the children into good order on nights like this is to let them help with the preparation – the easy bits – then give them leave to take whatever they like best. It works pretty well, though Becky tends to stand by the quiches and say "I made these" to all the guests.'

'And has she?'

'Say thirty per cent. And remember the pastry is supermarket frozen... It won't be long now before your mother rings to Australia.'

'Really? Won't it be early in the morning there?'

Pat looked sceptical.

'Dan told your mother when he first went out there that he got up at 5 a.m. every day to train. She took him at his word.'

'Wouldn't you?'

'Never. He is – pardon my French – a bullshit artist. He says what he thinks will impress people.'

'I'm getting a picture of my brother Dan.'

'To be fair, he has been horribly spoilt by your mother. After you were abducted she transferred all the love she'd been giving you to the youngest. That's what everybody says, anyway. Dan didn't have a chance.'

And half an hour later Kit saw Isla disappear into the hall, then heard her go upstairs. He guessed the phone had been transferred up there to give him a little privacy. Five minutes later his mother appeared at the door and beckoned.

'He's longing to talk to you,' she whispered. 'It's on the landing.'

Kit's inventiveness had left him. All he could think of to say when he took up the phone was: 'Hello, Dan.'

'Well, well, well. It's big brother Peter, returned from captivity.'

'It's Kit, and I had a very comfortable childhood, thank you.'

'I bet you did. I never went along with Mum's fears that you were being abused, starved, enslaved – you name it, she thought it was happening to you.'

'Why didn't you believe it? It's possible, horrible things happen.'

51

'Oh, I go my own way. Believe what I like.'

'Convenient for you.'

'Don't get sarky. There's no reason why we shouldn't be friends.'

'No, of course there's not. I don't remember anything about you.'

'Really? Well, I don't suppose I'd discovered football when you were snatched.'

'Probably not, since you were a baby. How's the career going in Oz?'

'Very nicely, thank you. It'll stand me in good stead when I get home. Which may be sooner than people think.'

'I look forward to that.'

'I bet you do. We can be friends, Peter–'

'Kit.'

'Kit, if that's what you want. We can be friends if you remember two things: keep your hands off my girlfriend, and keep your hands off my money.'

'By money you mean–'

'What's coming to me in my mother's will. Get it?'

'Oh, I get it.'

'What did you and Dan talk about?' his mother asked, when he went back to the party.

'Oh, just his hopes for the future and that,' said Kit vaguely, but not feeling at all vague.

In the taxi on the way home Isla said: 'There, now you know most of the family... The grandchildren are lovely, aren't they?'

Kit agreed, uncertain how far the implications of the analysis were meant to be understood by him. Whatever was the case he did understand them, and wondered at his birth mother feeling the need to make such base insinuations. The undercurrents in this family clearly ran strong.

CHAPTER THREE

Past History

When Kit went up to the enquiries office of the police headquarters in Leeds he was still largely unsure of what he wanted to see, who he should ask for, and how he should present himself and his case. He had spent the wakeful hours of his night in bed thinking over his new family, deciding they were a mixed bunch among whom he definitely disliked Dan and definitely liked Micky. Footballers these days – he remembered no earlier times – had a presumption of dislikeability stamped on their foreheads from even before their emergence from obscurity. He doubted very much whether Dan was ever going to make his emergence into footballing glory, and he had to admit he was glad of that. Dislikeability was all the better for not having instant fame and fortune attached to its coat-tails.

The sergeant at the desk was a middle-aged man, beginning to run to fat, a comfortable mix of geniality and firmness.

'Now, young man, what can I do for you?'

'It's a bit difficult,' mumbled Kit, conscious of not making a good impression. 'It concerns a kidnap that took place in 1989.'

'Before my time,' said the man, staring at his computer screen. 'What is it you want to report?... I suppose that's why you're here?'

'Yes... Yes, I suppose it is. It concerns the kidnapping of Peter Novello, who was three at the time.'

He was subjected to a concentrated stare.

'Oh? Kidnapping's pretty rare these days. Where did this one take place?'

'In Sicily.'

'Sicily? That explains it. Dicey sort of place in my experience. And what's the information you have that you want to report?'

'I am the child that was kidnapped. I lived at that time in Leeds with my mother whom I've now been reunited with, and my father, who is in a nursing home and I haven't met yet.'

'Ah... I wondered.' The stare was resumed momentarily, then he pressed some keys on his computer. 'Ah yes. I have it here... Well, you've done the right thing. Will you take a seat? Do you still answer to the name of Peter Novello?'

'Not as a rule,' said Kit, dallying by the desk in the vain hope of seeing anything on the screen. 'But I suppose I'll have to get used to it. The name I've always – nearly always – gone by is Christopher Philipson. Usually Kit.'

'Right. I'll give you a call when I've found someone to talk to you.'

Kit went and sat in a corner, looking around surreptitiously at the collected specimens of the indigent and the indignant gathered there. It was twenty minutes before a large man (once a sportsman, Kit guessed, but one no longer) came in, leant over the sergeant's desk, and had Kit pointed out to him. He came over, hand outstretched, and Kit felt obliged to submit to the finger-crunching ritual.

'Mr Novello? I'm Sergeant Hargreaves. Pleased to meet you. I'm not sure what we can do for you, but I've lined up an interview room, so come this way.' He ushered him through a door, taking them away from the public area, and then led him to a small office. 'I'm going to be starting from scratch here, so I wonder if you'd mind if we recorded the talk. It would give me a record to check things against if they get complicated – as I suspect they could.'

'I'd welcome it, and yes, they could get complicated. You realise I'll often be very vague myself...'

'Eh? Oh, I see. Being very young when it happened, I suppose. You probably don't have many memories of your time here.'

'Hardly any, and nothing very useful. I remember my father's feet, and my mother's smell when she took me in her arms – oh, and the smells of her cooking. Not very useful. And to tell you the truth I've got better memories of my bedroom – a real child's one, full of animals and cartoon characters.'

Hargreaves nodded and turned on the tape. For the next ten minutes Kit went over all his vague memories of his first family, of how everything had ended in Sicily and how the 'kidnap' had terminated with his being handed over to the Philipsons.

'A Glasgow family, you said,' Hargreaves muttered, perhaps relieved at hearing the last of the Sicilian end. 'So how did you get there?'

'Air, I think. I've just a memory of having flown when I was very young, and how I expected it to be exciting, and it wasn't.'

'You're not wrong,' said Hargreaves. 'Mostly cloud and things below impossible to pick out. Who was with you?'

'I don't remember. People I'd never seen before, I imagine, and never since either. Anyway I have no picture of them in my mind. A couple, that's all. Sort of couriers, I suppose.'

'That seems likely. Have you any memories of being left with the Philipsons?'

'None. The earliest remembrance from those early days is a bear in a tartan kilt, which I've probably still got in a cupboard somewhere.'

'You still live in the same house in Scotland?'

'Yes,' said Kit, feeling some need to apologise. 'I inherited everything when my new parents died. Only child, of course.'

'Ah, I thought you would be,' said Hargreaves. 'But people with children, or an only child, do adopt quite often – "to make the family complete" they usually say.'

'Adopt, yes. Take a kidnapped child as their own – I wouldn't have thought so.'

'Point taken. Now, do I understand that you gradually accepted the Philipsons as your own family – your birth family as they say these days?'

'Yes, I did,' said Kit at once. 'I must have asked about my birth mother at first, but she soon slipped out of my mind. I was so young. My memory of her – her smell when she kissed me – could have been anyone: grandma, maid, housekeeper – whoever.'

'And your new parents put it around that you were adopted?'

'In so far as they said anything, yes.'

'How far was that?'

'The two neighbours were the local people my mother knew best. I've talked to them in the weeks since she died. And she must have said something to her department at the University. Glasgow University. She had leave from them at first, then worked part-time and, when I was about twelve, went back to teach full-time.'

'Yes. So some people knew–'

'Or thought they knew. Yes. The woman next door said my mother informed her they were not going to tell me I was adopted till I was old enough to understand. That age was left vague, so the neighbour never took it up with me. She said she never thought twice about it.'

'Yes, people take adoption pretty much in their stride these days. You don't hear silly talk about "bad blood" anymore.' Sergeant Hargreaves stretched his long, tree-trunk legs under the table. 'Still, you came here, came down to Leeds, and found your real mother, knew where she was. So at some time you learnt or thought you did that you'd been adopted, and at some time, too, you learnt what had really happened was that you'd been abducted – am I right?'

Kit nodded.

'First things first: the adoption that never was. My mother, Genevieve Philipson, found she had breast cancer just over a year before she died. So she and I had that year together, knowing it would be her last, and making the best of it.'

'Your adoptive father was already dead?'

'Yes. Jürgen Philipson died five years ago. He was deputy editor of one of the Glasgow newspapers. Well, my mother and I used that year in all sorts of ways, but in particular I wanted to know about myself and my background. At first that meant the Philipsons, but I soon came upon something odd: in the family snap album there was only one snap of me as a baby. You'd have thought, having waited so long for a child, that they would have been snapping me all the time. Then I went over in my mind what I'd been told about myself as a baby, and I realised there was nothing. No stories about my first step, my first word. I had really come up with the answer to the mystery before my mother told me.'

'Ah, she did.'

'Yes. She thought I ought to know before she died. She was a fantastically truthful person, hated a lie. Yet she'd been living one for twenty years. One evening, when she'd gone to bed, in great pain, she told me that I was adopted, and I said I'd guessed as much. That pleased her. It meant that the lie had been less of a lie. I'd discovered the truth beforehand.'

'The truth?'

'Well, the fact that I had only come to them when I was three.'

'How much did she tell you that night?'

'Not much more than that I'd been adopted – only she said "you came to us", which must have been her love of truth asserting itself again – when I was three.'

'Didn't you ask questions?'

'Oh yes, we talked about things. I remember I nearly used the phrase "who I really was" once, but I caught myself in time and substituted "who I was for the first three years".'

'You have a good memory.'

'It was only a year ago – less. It was when the cancer really started to ... to bite. Poor Mother. She wanted to be brave, but often couldn't be. And there I was – always asking questions, suspecting she really knew the name of my birth mother. She fobbed me off with "the adoption people have a lot of rules and regulations" which didn't seem to tie in with the fact that people have a right to know the name of their birth father. In the end I told her – she loved the truth after all – that after her death I'd try to find out who my birth mother was.'

'How did she take that?'

'Not well at first. She wasn't thinking straight. When she could she realised that she couldn't stop me. And shouldn't. It was my right to try to find her, and she shouldn't put obstacles in my way. She only asked that I wouldn't do anything – act on the information, I mean – until after she was dead. I could say that without any difficulty. We were looking to fill every day when her illness allowed it to see or do something. I let my degree course lapse for the moment, with the university's permission, and we had as near to a whale of a time as was possible under the circumstances.'

'But what had she told you?'

'That my mother was a Mrs Novello, who lived in the Leeds area.'

'Nothing more than that? No Christian name or address? No reason why Mrs Novello had put you up for adoption after nurturing you for three years? That must be unusual.'

'Yes, I suppose it must be. Unless there's a sort of cumulative inability to cope, perhaps. Anyway that's what my mother told me. Do you think that at the time of the adoption – the handover, let's call it – she wanted to know as little as possible? That way she could not let anything slip, or have things forced out of her.'

'That's a bit melodramatic, isn't it?'

Kit shook his head.

'There's something I haven't told you: my adoptive father was a Jewish child refugee to England. He arrived by special train a week or two before war broke out. It could have been he who wanted to know as little as possible.'

'I suppose escaping Nazi Germany was bound to leave scars,' said Hargreaves, not able to hide a degree of scepticism.

'He left it when he was very young – hardly more than a baby. With his sister. I think he felt guilt, and the guilt built itself up as the world learnt more and more about what happened in the death camps. He and I did lots of things together, but he was never a happy person, except in his private life. In his professional life the death camps were a sort of shadow floating around and over him. He was always feeling he had to explain.'

'I see. And somehow this pair of people, intelligent, cultivated people – have I got it right...?'

'Oh yes. Very much so.'

'I'm not very cultivated myself, so I'm having difficulty connecting with them. This very cultured pair somehow connected up with people who were either prepared to kidnap to order – they wanted you – or who kidnapped and then sold you to the highest bidder.'

'Yes, it seems like that,' sighed Kit. 'I have difficulty in seeing the Philipsons as the highest bidders. But I suppose desperation could change things.'

'You mean they wouldn't stoop? I tell you, desperation changes almost everything. Well, there's nobody for you to ask now, is there?'

'No. Not so far as I know. I think I would have known if my mother had had some kind of confidant – someone she always told everything to.'

'Have you tried the newspapers?'

'Yes, the Scottish ones. That's where I saw the only reference to an abduction. It was a tiny paragraph in my father's paper, in one of those columns that rakes together this and that. It said that police in Leeds denied reports in a Sunday newspaper that the Novellos had received ransom demands after the abduction of ... and so on. About five lines, but that's how I learnt I'd been abducted. It seemed a strange way to learn.'

'I found that information just now in our file, of course. There wasn't a great deal more from newspapers, but I've taken copies for you. There's no reason you shouldn't have anything that's been in the press. At least the cuttings show you that you really never did become a national issue.'

He took out a red pen and circled small items in five different newspapers. None of them was a lead story by any means. The longest was two paragraphs.

'No,' said Kit ruefully. 'I'm not going to get a great deal from newspapers of the time.'

'I'm a bit surprised at that,' admitted Hargreaves. 'The Madeleine McCann case was exceptional, but still, "Angelic, fair-haired English toddler kidnapped in Mafia country" makes a pretty good story.'

'Yes, I suppose it does... It never felt at the time like I was being stolen. It felt like I was being found a new home. Because that's what they told me: a new home while my mother was ill.'

'Don't you remember anything else about "they"?'

'No, nothing. I was very young, remember.'

'Yes, of course. But I am surprised the newspapers didn't play up the possibility of your being taken by a paedophile ring or some such thing. It was a real possibility, after all... What is it you think we could do for you, sir?'

'Ah...' Even after all they'd just discussed Kit found it difficult to be specific. 'I'm not very clear in my head about that. I take it you've got nothing in the police file that could be DNA tested against my DNA?'

'No, nothing. You'd like to prove that you are who you think you are?'

'Something like that. Though no one in the Novello family has questioned that yet.'

'Try anything of the child's still in Seldon Road: furry animals, kiddies' books and so on. Both are possibilities, but lack of things to compare with is just typical of your problem: for us the kidnapping never became a case. We have on our files mostly bulletins from the Palermo police, translated over there, and sometimes quite incomprehensible. But in general I get the idea that they were telling us that they didn't want to know – or at least didn't want us to know. And we accepted that the crime took place on Italian soil, so it was mainly their affair. The Novello family never pushed hard for an investigation. So we did bugger all about it – pardon my Italian.'

'And yet there is this coincidence – let's call it that: I came back to British territory, flew back with an escort, with all the dangers of the crime being discovered as we all came through passport control or customs. Somehow, surely, there has to be a British dimension to this?'

'I think you're right. But we at the time knew nothing about that, of course.'

Hargreaves seemed to feel that the Leeds police had hardly distinguished themselves and needed to be apologised for.

'No, no... I'm going to see my birth father as soon as I can. He's where I got my name from – and possibly a lot more as well.'

'Novello. Not a common name, though a well-known one. There was a solicitor's firm with that name in it in Leeds at the time. Not primarily criminal stuff: wills, divorces, property disputes, compensation claims. Don't think it exists anymore.'

'That could be him. He's in an old people's home at the moment. People disagree about his condition, but they do seem to agree that he has lucid days, or comparatively lucid ones. It will be a bonus if he's having one when I go to see him, but I don't suppose they can be predicted.'

'I don't think we can be too much help to you there, sir. But I've just wondered–'

'Yes?'

'If the fact of your return will lead to new developments, new discoveries or revelations. That could bring a lot of tensions or worse into your little family. I think the best thing we can say at the moment is that we're aware of you, who you are – or claim to be – and we are interested in seeing the whole abduction matter finally settled. And there's something you could do, sir.'

'What's that?'

'You could make your connection to the police, your lifeline to us, known as widely as possible, particularly in your family.'

Kit frowned.

'You think my family were involved in my abduction? The Portuguese police initially thought that in the McCann case, didn't they? I always considered that was as unlikely as it's possible to get. Or do you think they'll gang up and get rid of me to stop me getting a share of the family's nest egg? They'd be absolutely top of any list of possible suspects, wouldn't they? I can see my brother Dan being stupid enough to get involved in that sort of plan, but none of the others.'

Hargreaves quietened him by waving a hefty fist.

'Maybe. I'm not expecting anything as

concrete as that. I'm just thinking what the situation is for your immediate family. They may all have wanted you to be found alive, but in their hearts they didn't expect that to happen.'

'Yes. My brother Micky said something along those lines,' said Kit.

'So now your miraculous reappearance may mean that the presumption of death is knocked for six, and maybe some well-laid plans based on that presumption are in danger of going the same way. That could put you in danger – see what I mean?'

'Yes, I do. But I'd bet my last quid against it,' said Kit. 'OK, I'll play up my closeness to the police. I'm a canny Scot, you know, by nature and nurture. I don't close any avenue.'

But walking out of the Millgarth police station, and then during a wander round the long aisles of Leeds Kirkgate Market close by, Kit thought – as he had done most of the last two nights – of himself and his relationship with his 'new' family. Would he bet his last pound on their being honest?

They had all seemingly coped well with his reappearance – all except Dan, and Kit didn't feel confident about Dan: how far were his reactions genuine, how far bravado or dramatisations aimed at making a macho impression? He'd know more when he actually met him. His mother had coped admirably, and so had Micky. His sister he was less sure of: perhaps Maria was the sort who never gave anything away, not easily anyway. And then there were Pat, Wendy (not yet part of the family, and probably never would be), Maria's husband Ivor, so far not met. He thought over this portrait gallery of family members, unsure of what puzzled him, but knowing something did.

As he was waiting at a bus stop it suddenly hit him. They were friendly, natural, interested in his return, but there was no warmth. No joy in having him back with them. They gave every sign that very soon all their lives would go back to being pretty much what they had been hitherto. There should have been, in their reception of him, something of relief, of delight. Yet even in his mother Kit sensed that the expected emotions were missing.

Something was wrong.

CHAPTER FOUR

Father and Son

'Mr Novello – it's your visitor.'

The head cleaner at the Four Bells Nursing Home had received him very kindly and walked him along to room number 16, telling him, as she probably told every visitor she opened the door to, that the four bells referred to were the bells of four nearby churches – no doubt comforting reminders of the Four Last Things. The cleaner had opened the door, and Kit had caught the briefest of glimpses of an old man sitting in an armchair before he was on his feet and pottering around to get tea ready.

'Ah yes. Now you'll have a cup of tea, won't you? I know you want to talk to me, though I can't think why. Just an ordinary solicitor, sometimes defending people in court, but mostly trying to take the sting out of death and divorce and all the other nightmares the flesh is heir to.' His face beamed a smile of self-satisfaction. 'That wasn't bad, was it? Go down well in court. They say I'm losing my mind, but... Here's milk and sugar. I gave up sugar, like everyone else.

Can't think why. Right, now take a seat. Oh ... you have. Now what did you say your name was?'

Kit was watching him closely. He was a tall, lean figure, rather more Scandinavian than Italian, but his Italian blood would be well diluted after the family's years in Britain. Or did the Novellos in any case come from the Germanic north of Italy? Kit noted every movement the old man made in his pottering, and decided that there was a strong strain of performance in him. He was a bumbler but he was acting out a bumbler too, a stage version. It seemed to be for his own amusement, but no doubt it acted as some kind of cover as well. The smile on his face as he went about this business was a secret one, not welcoming, but full of self-love and self-congratulation.

'My name when you knew me was Peter Novello,' Kit said.

The old man nodded.

'Ah,' he said. 'One of my tribe.'

He took out the teeth which Kit had already identified as false and gave them a perfunctory polish on his shirt, then put them back in his mouth.

'Not just your tribe,' said Kit. 'One of your own family. I am the son of Frank and Isla Novello.'

The claim did not produce any kind of earthquake.

'Oh, I don't think so,' Frank Novello said. 'I have a son, and I know Michael – see him often. And Dan is in Australia I believe. I hear all about him. Oh no, you've got that one wrong.' He took a large gulp at his tea. 'But that's enough about you. Let's talk a bit about me.'

It was when he said this, with a steely glint in his eye, that Kit knew he was being played with. The mind may have been decaying, but it was the remains of a trained legal mind.

'That suits me fine,' Kit said. 'It's what I came for. Tell me about your early life.'

'Oh dear – most unmemorable, you might say dull as ditchwater. Private school – not because I failed the eleven-plus, but because my parents confused it with a public school. I'd have been better off at a state school, but I got into university, studied law, and my parents bought me into a solicitor's practice.'

'Where was this?'

'Oh, Leeds mostly. I've always had a strong sense of place, and I knew all along that my place was Leeds. Connections sometimes took me elsewhere, but I'd say eighty per cent of my business was local.'

'What sort of people were your parents?'

'Conventional people: my father Italian-British, but more the latter than the former. Singing "O Sole Mio" was about as Italian as he got. My mother was a pretty little local girl. It was really quite a happy home.'

'And so when you married you tried to set up a similar close family?'

'If you say so,' he said, and then, thinking perhaps that he sounded cynical, perhaps even Machiavellian, he added: 'We tried at any rate, Isla and I. But as I'm sure you know, it ended in separation, then divorce.'

'But you were Catholics?' Kit asked. The old man shrugged.

'There's degrees of Catholicism these days as in everything else. You know Italians have 0.9 of a child per family? My Catholicism, like theirs, was of a pretty low degree.'

'Why did you and Isla separate?'

'Why does any couple? We grew apart. Sounds horticultural, doesn't it? Next question.'

'Was the growing apart caused by the abduction of your child?'

'That's a supplementary, not a new question. In any case I can't answer it because I don't know what you're talking about.'

'You must surely know that one of your sons was abducted while you and your family were on holiday in Sicily in 1989?'

'Don't remember anything of the sort. Next question.'

'Can I just tell you something?' Kit asked. He found himself looking at a lump of carved stone rather than a face of flesh and blood but he carried on. 'I came back to Leeds three days ago, and went straight to see my ... to see my mother. She was delighted to see me, and accepted me at once.'

'Accepted you? What as? The Tichborne claimant?'

'I'm afraid I don't know who the Tichborne claimant is.'

'A nineteenth-century imposter who passed himself off as someone he wasn't in an attempt to claim a large inheritance. He failed.'

'I have no interest in money, no desire to push your other children aside. I have already inherited enough for my needs, and in any case I'm not your eldest son.'

He sounded, even to himself, priggish. Novello sneered.

'You're not any kind of son. Do you imagine anything Isla thinks, or anything she does or does not accept, has any influence on me? We separated fifteen or more years ago, and I've never done a better thing. If I had any religion I'd give daily thanks that I decided on it. She has money – money she had from me at the time of the divorce – and she does with it what she likes. Makes it grow, I'd guess, knowing her. Whether I accept your preposterous story is irrelevant to you, and I assure you is something that is never going to happen.'

'I see,' said Kit, adding: "What are you afraid of?'

'Of being bored out of my mind by getting involved in a futile and dubious controversy. Isn't it time you were going?'

'If you want me to,' said Kit. 'By the way, I haven't mentioned I have memories of you.'

'Bully for you.'

'I have memories of your feet, in soft slippers which you had trodden down at the heel.'

'Photograph all the old men in this hell-hole and I guarantee three-quarters of them will have similar slippers to these.' He kicked his feet out towards Kit, crowing at the downtrodden nature of their heels. Kit began to gather together his things, watched by a sardonically grinning father. 'Didn't get what you wanted, did you?'

'No,' said Kit, proffering his hand. It was ignored. He shrugged and went to the door. When it was opened and he himself halfway through it he heard the old man in the chair shouting: 'Come again soon.' And as the door shut on the father of his memories he heard: 'But not too soon.'

Outside in the corridor Kit rested his briefcase on a small table and took a great breath of nursing home air into his lungs. That had not been the reunion with his father he had been preparing himself for emotionally. It was as if something – a box of delicious chocolates perhaps – had been snatched away from him at the last moment.

'In one of his moods, was he?'

The voice was that of the plump, comfortable woman who had brought him to his father's room. It was hardly more than ten minutes ago, but he was glad to see her again. He shook his head.

'I suppose that's what it was. He denied knowing who I was, denied having a son who was abducted–'

'That's you, is it?'

'Yes. I was abducted in Sicily when I was three. After denying the facts he more or less threw me out, and called after me, "Come again soon." Is he mad in the clinical sense, rather than "mad" in the sense of pretty strange?'

'Search me. I just clean and do odd jobs. He's done this before, with people he had no strong connection with: former clients, a partner, that kind of thing. Maybe it's just his sense of humour. Reacting against years in a dull and despised job.'

Kit thought this through, and thought it an intelligent suggestion.

'Maybe you're right. If only I'd had a bit longer...'

'Since he said "come again" you could do just that. Well, I'd better be–'

But she was interrupted by the door of his father's room opening, and a red and cross face peering out.

'Where's some more hot water for my tea, woman? By the time you bring it it'll be stone cold. Stop talking to strange men and do your bloody job.'

He slammed the door shut. The cleaner smiled at Kit and went into the kitchen. Kit raised his hand, then put the atmosphere and smell of the nursing home behind him.

He gave an account of the nursing home visit the next day when he had lunch in the Vesper Gate near Kirkstall Abbey with Micky. It was well rehearsed and orderly because he had already put together an account of it for Sergeant Hargreaves. His elder brother justified his reputation by picking unenthusiastically at a hamburger, obviously preferring the accompanying chips. Kit ate a prawn salad, knowing that he would be eating with Isla that night. The account did not take long, since the visit had been such a short one. Micky kept nodding, with a sort of delight on his face.

'Yes, he'd do that when I started going to see him. Denied ever having seen me before, denied having been married and had children – then dredging up memories of us all as young kids.'

'Us all?' Kit queried.

'Well, no, I can't remember that he ever mentioned you, Kit. But think: you'd been out of the family's ken for years by then.'

'Perhaps you could jog his memory next time you go.'

'I'll do that, but it'll have to be done carefully. He knows if you have something you want from him and he clams up, determined not to give it.'

'What do you think of that cleaner's notion that he's compensating for a very dull professional life?'

'I like it... Or at least, I rather wonder whether he hasn't been doing that all his life.'

'What makes you say that?'

Micky thought, then asked a question.

'What did he tell you about his practice as a lawyer?'

'He said it consisted of dull stuff – divorce, wills, broken contracts and so on, or that's what I understood him to be saying. All centring on Leeds, naturally.'

'Yes,' said Micky, who'd got the answer he expected. 'But even in the last years of his living with us in Seldon Road, the thing we children noticed was how seldom he was with us. He was doing a hell of a lot of business in somewhere that wasn't Leeds – that's what I think now, anyway.'

'Why not some other obliging lady kept in a snug little flat in Headingley or Pudsey?'

'I don't think he'd have done it in Leeds,' said Micky thoughtfully. 'My understanding of him is that all his professional life he was a cautious man – hiding his less respectable, less professional sides. A fancy woman in some other Northern town – well yes, maybe. All very discreet it would have been... The thing is, I have a memory–'

'Yes?'

'It must have been the first two or three years after he moved out of Seldon Road and before he ditched us as a family. He dropped us, and my memory is that we children didn't mind very much. Still, it left a gap, and it left us with a lot of questions we'd like to have asked but never got a chance to.'

'Yes – I know the feeling,' said Kit.

'Anyway, it must have been in those two years or so when there was still some contact with us children, and I was walking with him in the centre of Leeds – Park Row I think it was, and we were on the way from a pizza together to a rugby league game – anyway, someone grabbed his arm, and said, "Hi, Frank, what are you doing in Leeds? I phoned you last week and they said you were on vacation."'

'That must have been a surprise,' said Kit.

'I thought it must have been a mistake – he'd mistaken Dad for someone else. But then I remembered he'd got the Christian name right. And then my dad gestured to me to go a few feet away, and he immediately began a hush-hush conversation with this man: heads lowered to be closer together, voices very low, me and the rest of Leeds shut out. I heard nothing of what they said beyond a few words: it was all lost in the roar of the traffic coming from City Square.'

'But what did you make of it?' Kit asked.

'I didn't, frankly. But for some reason – I suppose because it turned my dad into a man of mystery – the incident remained in my mind, and when we tried to understand why the divorce had meant we kept one parent and lost the other (we all knew kids at school who'd had parents divorced but kept good contact with both), that meeting surfaced in my mind, and we kids discussed it without getting very far.'

'So Maria and Dan knew of it?'

'Oh yes. It was part of our family folklore. Not that we got anywhere finding a meaning for it, like I say.'

'What did you decide?'

'Me, the one who saw it, and so really the one in the best position to understand it, I decided my father was running a double life, but it was a professional life, not an emotional or sexual one.'

'I've never heard of solicitors who played away from home in their professional lives,' said Kit. 'It sounds rather unlikely.'

'Fair enough. What did I know about life, professional or emotional? I was eleven or twelve.'

'What do you really think about your dad now?'

Micky shrugged.

'Like I say: what do I know? I was ten or so, I think, when he left us, so I have a fair number of early memories: Christmases, games of cricket, holidays. Since then I have these few fragments of memory like the one I've just mentioned, and then the experience of visiting him for the last two years, when I can't make out how mad he is, or how sane. I'm playing in the dark.'

'And what is your guess?'

Micky thought.

'I've tried to exclude anything said by Mum, and truth to tell she doesn't say a great deal about him. But one thing she always comes back to if his name comes up is: "He's selfish. It's self, self, self all the time, and no one else is allowed to get a look-in." I can imagine that's true. He plays with people. When he played with you yesterday, was there any sign of his regretting those little games before you left? No, I thought not. Just relish at having had a good time. It's the same with the rest of the family: we were cast off because we were no use in his self-promotional efforts.'

'Is our mother a good judge of character?'

Micky laughed.

'Not bad. But I was just thinking that if you lump her in with the family, she's no shirker in the selfishness stakes herself. She lives for the family, but she expects them to live for her too. She'll always give advice, sometimes in the form of commands. She doesn't like it if the advice isn't followed, but what gets her goat is if they go away and do something without consulting her at all. Then you really feel the sting of the family whip. But I've got to say I love her like every boy is said to love his mother, but very seldom does.'

'She kept you all together.'

'Yes, she did. Even with her favouritism of Dan – always finding excuses for him, with the excuses becoming even more outrageous than the offences – it was she who kept us all from marking him down as hopeless. We know in our hearts that he is never going to make anything of himself, but we don't bring that out into the open because it would hurt Mum so much. And who am I, anyway, to criticise him for not making anything of himself?'

'You seem to have made yourself a very nice job and a lovely family.'

'The job is menial – painting and decorating, specialising in Old Leeds. Scrape off the Artex, paste up the classical shades. As to family, that falls mainly on Pat. I had to marry a strong-minded woman, otherwise I'd have been nothing.'

'I don't believe that.'

Micky pushed his plate away, the hamburger three-quarters uneaten. Kit put his knife and fork over the remains of his salad. He could never bear not-quite-ripe continental tomatoes. He sat for some time in thought. Micky left him to his meditations, then finally said: 'Is there anything else you want to know, Kit?'

'I don't think so... But it's really the overall picture I can't get clear in my head. Was I abducted, and then after a time nobody much cared? Things went on here more or less as before, so maybe my name hardly ever came up.'

'No,' protested Micky. 'It wasn't like that at all. Mum cared enormously. I'm sure you've sensed that. Dad certainly less so, but he had a job, and getting ahead, to take his mind off the abduction. What you're forgetting is, the rest of us were children. The family couldn't revolve around the one of us that wasn't there. What would Maria and me have thought if no one asked us what we'd been doing at school that day, or what we wanted to do over the weekend? Dan was too young for that, of course, but he had even more needs than the rest of us.'

'Things had to go on as usual, you mean?'

'Course they did. That's why it seems like we forgot you, though I'm quite sure we didn't. And for the older generation you were remembered the whole time – always in their thoughts, as they say on funeral wreaths.'

'In Mother's thoughts maybe,' said Kit. 'You've admitted the same couldn't be said for Dad. I think he was quite happy to forget me.'

'Well, not that exactly, but ... yes ... he didn't feel it like Mum did, that I would admit...' He shifted uneasily in his chair. 'There's something I haven't told you.'

'What's that?'

'This friend who Dad met by chance in town, when we were on our way to the league game... What he actually said was: "I phoned you last week in Glasgow." I didn't know where Glasgow was, or probably how to spell it, but I swear that's what he said.'

CHAPTER FIVE

Used-Car Salesman

That evening Kit went round to his mother's house in Seldon Road. Isla cooked a three-course meal – pasta, veal and sauté potatoes and deliciously, fattening dessert. The meal landed bang between the Italian and the English, and was not unlike meals his adoptive mother, who worshipped Italy, had cooked during his adolescence. He had been uneasy when he arrived at the house because he was conscious of eyes watching him from neighbouring windows. The meal made him feel more at home. Isla ate early, so as to have the meal done and washed up. Afterwards they sat and watched *Jubilee Terrace* on the television. The landlord of the Duke of York's was heading for a disastrous love affair, and Dawn Kerridge was dabbling in sex-for-money.

'I'm not sure I should have let you watch that,' said Isla, only half joking.

'If I can't watch *Jubilee Terrace*, what is there left I can watch?' asked Kit, laughing. 'You forget I'm years out of short trousers. I'm twenty-two.'

Isla sighed.

'How I wish I could have seen you in short trousers, on your first day at school.'

'I don't remember much about my first day, except that I liked school very much. I remember better a day three weeks later, when they put me up into a higher class because they said I was so bright. I created blue murder.'

'Why? It sounds like a compliment.'

'It was. But I liked Miss Ockham who was form mistress of first year, and I didn't like Mrs Sullivan who was mistress of second year. And I'd just begun to make friends, and I had to begin the whole process of acclimatisation all over again.'

'You've had to do an awful lot of that in your short life,' said Isla, her feelings easily touched. Kit looked at her with pity in his gaze, but also with the idea of putting her right.

'You sound as if you want to apologise. You don't have to. In fact you can't apologise – not for something you had no control over. And I'm not sure that what I did with the Philipsons was that – acclimatisation, I mean. Genevieve was a "second mummy", so I called her that naturally. I can't really remember but I imagine that you and all the others here just became less and less vivid in my mind until you were gone from it completely. I should be the one who does the apologising, barring the fact that I was only three at the time.'

Isla sighed and wiped her eyes.

'Did you like school later on as well?'

'I loved it. And I did well. I expect if I hadn't done well I wouldn't have loved it. I'm like that.'

Isla thought.

'Do you know, you're the only one of my children who did well at school? Maria was competent, just about in the top half, but she never enjoyed learning, or took much away from the lessons. I think she was just waiting to start life proper. And I suppose you could say the same for Micky, and poor Dan.'

'Why "poor Dan"? He gives the impression of being very much in control.' Kit described this as an impression because he didn't think it was anything more substantial.

'But I wouldn't call football "life proper", would you?' said Isla. And Micky tells me Dan's not good enough ever to do really well.'

'He's still a teenager. He'll grow up some time. He'll have to. And perhaps that will be better than earning massive sums for just kicking a ball around.'

'I don't think Dan will feel like that. And these days you don't have to grow up, even when reality is staring you in the face. You can take drugs, fritter your life away and die early. You know all about that, I expect, coming from Glasgow. I just hope Dan will be able to take disappointment if that's what he's going to get in his footballing life. Then he can make a real choice, do some work, make a good life for himself.'

Kit didn't feel confident of that, so he just nodded. For a few minutes there was a companionable silence, and then Isla said: 'You've been to see your father, haven't you?'

'Yes, I have.' There was another silence, less companionable, then he asked: 'Does that upset you?'

'No... Well, yes. But I knew that's what you'd want to do – would have to, just to say you'd seen him. How was he?'

Kit told her the truth, not necessarily what she wanted to hear.

'Not too bad – quite OK physically. I'm not sure I could make a judgement about the mental side. I didn't understand him – didn't get him.'

'What do you mean?' Isla looked worried.

'I didn't know whether he was playing with me: for example, whether he had really forgotten that he'd ever had a son called Peter.'

'Is that what he tried to say? What a cruel way of playing with you! But I expect that's what it was: just a sort of game. Sadistic. You know he never thought you'd be found. He said Sicilian gangsters knew what they were doing. I thought it was a horrible way of putting it.'

'I don't know if it was true.'

'Frank said that you had probably been killed during the kidnap, or when they were escaping from the island.'

'The kidnap was very peaceful. Quite subtle, really. I was just led away. Strange that I remember that. No Sicilian gangsters to get the ransom money and then deliver my corpse.'

'Oh don't!'

'If my father was playing with me in pretending not to know who I was and what I wanted, then that really was cruelty. Why would he want to be cruel to his own child? Did he hate me? How could he hate a child of three? Is he like that?'

'No... I'm sure it's not that... He just hates to be disappointed – he looks on the dark side because he says things usually do turn out worse than people hope.'

'Hmmm. I got the impression he was enjoying himself.'

'Maybe. It's possible. He used to go in for this black humour, which I can't see is humour at all. And people don't like it. His clients didn't.'

'He says he only took boring cases, so that may have meant he had mostly boring clients.'

'I shouldn't think that was true. He was earning a bomb by the time we separated. Lots of work in other parts of the country. People came to him for his special knowledge – whatever it was. I could never make head nor tail of it when he tried to explain it, which he didn't like doing... So your dad wasn't as funny in the head as Micky makes out?'

'It may have been a good day for him. The staff there seemed used to his ways. It's a good home.'

'Oh, he'd have insisted on that. He likes his comforts, or used to. In the home someone else does the work and he lives like a lord.'

'That's my impression,' said Kit, thinking of the staff nurse. 'Now all I have to do is get him to accept who I am.'

Isla hesitated before she said: 'Do be careful. Don't get too close to your father. It's a recipe for heartbreak.'

'Maybe,' said Kit. 'But I'd hate not to try.'

Isla withdrew at once.

'I'm sorry. Forget what I said. The last thing I'd want is to put you against your father.'

But you already have, thought Kit. *Or tried to.*

'I'd just like to know what makes him tick,' he said.

'Wouldn't we all?' said Isla sourly. 'A

90

sadistic taste for upsetting other people I'd say.'

'Thank you for not putting me against my father,' said Kit. The two looked at each other, and then burst out laughing. But it was uneasy laughter.

Later in the evening Isla suggested that he stop the night: she'd had a full-sized bed moved into the old nursery. Kit had intended to accept when this was offered, as it was bound to be before too long, but now he found that he did not want to. The conversation about his father had cast a cloud, though he could not pinpoint why. If anyone knew his father it should be his mother.

'I won't tonight,' he said. 'I've got to make a quick trip to Glasgow. It'll only be a couple of days. At most three. I'll book out of my hotel here tomorrow morning, then when I come back I'll stay here.'

'That will be nice,' said Isla, concealing her disappointment behind a buoyant tone. 'Where will you stay in Glasgow?'

Kit's face expressed his surprise.

'My home, of course. The place where I grew up.'

'I forgot. You've still got your ... home there.'

Kit's decision to go home for a few days was a decision of the moment, but it had been meditated almost since he had arrived in Leeds. He was not by nature a large-city man, but he wanted to go back to Glasgow because he had unfinished business there. Or rather, he had unfinished business all over the place, and probably he would find that all those pieces of business were interconnected. But for the moment he wanted to concentrate on the one question: how did the small boy who was abducted in Sicily land up in Glasgow? The obvious answer was: because in Glasgow there was a middle-aged family wanting a child.

That by itself did not get him far. What connection was there between the newspaper editor's family in Glasgow and the gang (Mafia? Camorra? Independent crooks?) who had taken him from his mother? What link was there between Glasgow and Sicily? It was far from obvious.

When he said goodbye to his mother that night he asked her: 'Isla, what were you doing when I was kidnapped?'

'What was I–? Oh, I see what you mean. I was fetching you an ice cream from the little van along the road from the hotel. Pineapple. You loved pineapple. *Dolce di ananas*. There was a queue waiting, not more than six or seven people, mostly parents getting them for their kiddies, so I waited, and the queue went quickly because we all wanted more or less the same thing. I wasn't away more than five minutes – less than ten anyway. But when I got back – oh God! You must blame me. What was I doing, leaving a child of three on his own like that?'

'Where was I?'

'In the little garden of the hotel. It was called the Hotel Siciliana. Will you ever–?'

'Forgive you? Nothing to forgive. I've had a good life, and intend to have more of the same thing for the next fifty or sixty years. Goodnight, Mum. I'll see you in a day or two, and I'll bring some things that can stop in the nursery for my visits. I like to think of its being occupied again.'

And when he kissed her goodnight it was with most of the warmth back in his heart that he had felt for her on the first day.

The next morning at breakfast Kit was in for a surprise. Breakfast was traditional in the Hutton Hotel in Headingley, and he was just reaching for a piece of toast to round off a gargantuan feast when he was conscious of a tall figure coming and planting itself on the empty table beside him. He looked up and saw a lean figure with an outstretched hand and a sharp purposeful eye.

'You must be Kit. Or Peter.'

'Kit will do. How did you know?'

'You're the only person under fifty in this room.'

'And you are?'

'Ivor Battersby. Your brother-in-law.' They

shook hands. He was a man in his late forties, obviously capable and certainly making every effort to be friendly and welcoming – or to appear to be. 'I got your hotel from Isla. I hope that's all right?'

'Of course it is. I want to get to know the family. And, of course, I want people to contact me if they have anything to tell me that might be helpful.'

'About how you came to be a Glasgow boy instead of a Leeds one? I wish you luck. Whether you're likely to get any information is another matter, but I hope you do. Look – I've got the morning off until twelve o'clock and I can run you to the station when we're done. I thought we ought to get to know each other, and we can pick up Maria somewhere along the way, or go for a coffee with her back at the house. Is that too boring a prospect?'

'It sounds just what I need to have.'

So he settled his hotel bill, fetched his packed suitcase from his room, and went with this forceful, slightly brash man to his waiting Mercedes.

'I thought I'd show you some of the suburbs. Either you've seen the centre of Leeds over and over or you will do if you keep up the connection with us here, so you need to see some of the outlying places – see more than just Headingley and Kirkstall. The fact that most of my business interests are there is a sort of bonus for me. I can swank and be informative at the same time.'

'Why have you shunned the centre?' said Kit, clicking in his seat belt.

'Because the centre doesn't cater any more for the ordinary person's ordinary needs. Well, Leeds Kirkgate Market does maybe, but otherwise – zilch. You'd think there'd be a butcher's, wouldn't you? Town this size? It's market, or supermarket, or nothing. Fishmonger's, then? Fish is no longer cheap, but more and more popular. No, it's market or supermarket or nothing. And so it goes on. And the market becomes less and less market-like year by year, with video shops, DVDs, computers. So you go to the suburbs to get a bargain, to get a specialised service, to do deals in the old style and not get fleeced.'

They had driven through Horsforth, and now turned into a side street with nothing particular to mark it off.

'See that garage? That's mine. One of a chain of eight. Each one has a used-car division, with specialised interests: old bangers, environmentally friendly ones, high-mileage-to-the-litre ones, totally reli-able and boring ones – you name what you want and we send you to the right branch, or sell it to you sight unseen. They trust us so much that that often happens. It's the same with the chain of shops we have.

Corner shops you might call them, but each one is carefully positioned and each one has a specialisation...'

Kit settled back into his conducted tour. Truth to tell, he was enjoying it, as listening to a committed enthusiast often is fascinating, even if the actual sums quoted and the turnover rehearsed so thoroughly they could be gabbled through were not in themselves gripping. Ivor was a vivid describer and self-publicist, and if Kit tired of the man's subject matter he could look at the churches and railway stations, the streets of still-grimy houses, the agricultural land stretching into the distance – of no interest to Ivor because it contained too few customers and competitors.

At eleven o'clock, having dismissed the idea of a drink in a pub, Ivor arranged things so they cruised into the drive of his house – brick with portico, designed with a total misunderstanding of the classical models that the bits were intended to ape.

'Home sweet home,' said Ivor. 'Maria will have coffee on the make. It's her time for it.'

And she did. She was dressed informally but in the sort of blouse and skirt that said they didn't come from a mass-market chain. She kissed Kit, sat him down in a chair that embraced and welcomed him, and put before him a plate of cake and biscuits.

'Let's not talk about garages and shops,'

she said. 'I get enough of that, particularly as I act as relief or deputy manager in situations of emergency. Tell me about you. What's happened since we met?'

So he told them about the slight fluctuations in his relationship with his birth mother, his visit to the police, his talk with Micky, and at last the visit to the nursing home and his birth father.

'So how was Dad?' asked Maria. 'Mad as a meat axe?'

'Respect the old,' said Ivor. 'I have a vested interest.'

'In any case, he isn't – or wasn't on the day I met him – mad, so far as I could see,' said Kit. 'But definitely odd. Playful, sadistic, wanting to gain and maintain a position of superiority, of his being in charge. Interest in me there was, even as he denied knowing me or knowing of me, but concern for me in any human way there certainly wasn't.'

'He doesn't have a reputation for warmth and concern,' said Ivor.

'I think I could have guessed that from Micky's account of how he dropped contact with his children. Apparently as soon as he decided they weren't all that bright – sorry Maria, I was thinking of the boys – and didn't add anything to his image, he just forgot about them.'

'Yes, he did,' his sister said. 'It didn't affect me that much but Micky was very hurt. As a teenager I would naturally have gone to Mum with my problems, but the boys had to do likewise because there was no adult male around any longer. If they'd rung to say they wanted to talk to him they'd have been given an appointment time, same as anyone else. If he didn't charge them it was because it would get around and he would be the subject of ridicule. He likes sarcasm and ridicule when he directs it at others, but he hates it when others direct it at him.'

'Sarcasm and ridicule, though, were very effective in his job,' said Ivor. 'The less human feeling he had about a case, the more effective his use of sarcasm and ridicule was.'

'I've had two conflicting views of him as a lawyer,' said Kit. 'One was of him as essentially a Leeds man, doing boring, routine solicitors' jobs – wills, family disputes, divorce settlements. The other is of him frequently away on lucrative legal business. He seems to have had two distinct careers.'

'That's right. He did,' said Ivor.

'How do you know about him?' Kit asked. 'From Maria?'

Maria shook her head.

'Not from me. We kids were completely in the dark. Suited us. He was out of our lives.'

Ivor sat for a few moments in thought.

'I think I've always known *of* him – known his name. I only got to know what he did for the really lucrative part of his profession at the time I began going with Maria. People started coming up to me and filling me in with the gossip.'

'Why? To warn you off her?'

'No, I don't think so. I think they meant well by me, felt I ought to know what the gossip said so I would know what I was getting into. It was, I thought, nothing very dreadful.'

'Who were the people? What real knowledge of him did they have?'

Ivor Battersby shifted in his seat.

'If you're in the used-car business you get to know some pretty dodgy individuals – without, of course, being dodgy yourself necessarily, and I'm not.'

'Of course you're not,' said Kit grinning.

'Many of the salesmen are petty crooks wanting to go straight – after a jail sentence, for example, or after a lucky heist that's given them the wherewithal to quit a way of life that's risky and not all that profitable. So I learnt that what Frank Novello had built up over the years was a close rapport with the world of gang crime.'

Kit thought for a bit.

'What does that mean? That he was good at defending them when they were on trial? Everyone should have a good defence lawyer, and there's no shame at being good at getting a client off.'

'No...o...o. He was good at defending them, good at finding loopholes, ambiguities in laws and Acts of Parliament. But that's not all of it, or even half. First of all, he became very close to the gang leaders in Manchester, especially as a negotiator in territorial disputes, in disputes about the various kinds of criminal practices, and sometimes in purely personal matters – disputes over girlfriends and so on.'

'Go on,' said Kit.

'I know someone who originally encountered him in a divorce suit, his own, then in an adjudication between rival gangs who had been at loggerheads about the geographical limits of their sway. He said it was like Frank was two different people. In the first he was caustic, wry, using ridicule and character assassination. He was a different man with the representatives of the gangs – this was in Liverpool. He was emollient, genial, the born peacemaker. My friend said you could see why he was in demand in the areas where gangs operated – London, Manchester...'

'Glasgow?' hazarded Kit. Ivor smiled.

'Oh yes. Definitely Glasgow.'

'The ice cream wars?'

'Those are what everyone has heard about. They're a small part of the story. There were pizza wars, wars identified by the names of the gang leaders. I didn't want to mention Glasgow because I didn't want to put ideas into your head – ideas that I couldn't prove or disprove. It's not something that interests me. And I came into Frank Novello's story quite late. When Maria and I married he was drawing to the end of his career – both sides of it.'

'You never talked it over with him?'

Ivor looked at him.

'I've never met him. He wasn't even at our wedding.'

'I'm beginning to think I'm not the only child my dad doesn't want to acknowledge,' said Kit.

'That's right,' said his sister. 'Remember, it goes both ways. We don't acknowledge him. Have nothing to do with him. That suits Ivor down to the ground because a garage owner doesn't want any connection with anyone whose activities are dicey.'

'I'm not sure peacemaking is a dicey activity,' said Kit.

'Well, when gang warfare is in the equation it sure as hell involves players who aren't on the side of law and order,' said Ivor, getting up. 'Come on, I'll take you to the station. Glasgow awaits.'

CHAPTER SIX

No Place Like it

'Well, this is cosy,' said George Farson, a neighbour from down the road, stretching out his feet and sipping as if his life depended on it. 'But I feel a fraud. I knew your mother to gossip with in the street, but hardly more than that. Gossiped about other people, never her, or me come to that. Brought her a few old magazines when I knew she ... hadn't got long. You know, I don't think any of us knew her really well. I don't think she wanted people to know that much about her.'

Kit knew he was right. He looked around the family living room at the motley assembly of academics, neighbours and kindred spirits. Sniffing the atmosphere (with its mixture of pipe smoke, defiantly indulged in, high-mindedness and sheer love and admiration), he thought he detected, too, an overlay of embarrassment – that they were almost under his roof under false pretences, though the pretences were not theirs but his. The thought made him wonder, briefly, if he had ever known his parents well. He had walked round Waverley Street and the adjoining thoroughfares in the early evening sunshine the day after his return and had noticed places where his mother sometimes visited, people he knew she respected (she could hardly confide in people she did not respect). He had then gone through her address book to find Glasgow people she seemed to be close to, and perhaps to trust. But all in all the little sherry party that resulted had amounted to no more than twelve people, only four of whom were well acquainted. Could anything possibly come of it?

Kit had bought, under advice, the best sherry he could find. That was something his mother had always insisted upon. You didn't serve cheap plonk to your friends. You served them the best you could afford.

'I think you may be right about my mother,' said Kit to George, conscious that he was more relaxed about using that word about the mother who'd raised him than he was about his birth mother in Leeds. 'But it's probably just a matter of temperament, isn't it? My mother was reserved – full stop. She wasn't willing to share personal matters with people she had a casual relationship with. It made her seem secretive, when perhaps she was not.'

'She was renowned in the department for being ... let's call it discreet.'

The man who had joined the pair of them was one of the few that Kit knew fairly well. He was Professor Purbright, the head of the Fine Arts Department at Stevenson University – his mother's ex-boss, and by and large a respected one. He was clutching an unlit pipe, though whether as a political statement, or as an old man's equivalent of Linus's blanket, Kit was unsure.

'She put everything she had into her academic duties, then when they were done she was off – clutching her briefcase stuffed with heavy art books, marking, the latest numbers of art periodicals. There was never any doubt that her family came first. She'd told me once – a rare moment of speaking about her private life – that if there was ever any question of a divided loyalty – say if you or Jürgen had some physical or mental problem – she would resign the lecturing hours immediately and give her all to home. "I don't do it for the money," she said, "only to keep my brain alive."'

'That sounds like Genevieve,' said Kit. 'And I'm sure she would have done just that. In fact, when my father was ill she contemplated resigning, but he begged her not to. She was coasting towards retirement age, and as he'd been given a death sentence he thought she'd be making a pointless sacrifice. He knew she wouldn't be any good as a terminal nurse, and he wouldn't be any good as a terminal patient.'

'We knew almost as little about Jürgen as we did about you,' said Professor Purbright.

'He was as discreet, as unpersonal, as Genevieve,' said Kit. 'But I would think her colleagues were bound to be interested in the sudden arrival of a three-year-old child.'

'Oh, they were surprised. As you say, that was natural. But as they were sensitive, academic types they held back, mostly. I do remember one time – the only time – when one of the staff tried to get something out of Genevieve. We were having a staff pub crawl after work at the end of oral exams, and we knew that you, Kit, were at a camp in the Lake District and Jürgen was away – sister ill or something. So we pressured Genevieve and for once she accepted our invitation – "half an hour" she insisted it had to be. And one of our staff members – she was thinking of adopting, was Edith Currie ... you wouldn't know her, Kit – she asked your mother if she thought adopted children made for bigger problems.'

'What did my mother say?'

'She said your adoption was a bit out of the ordinary, but certainly you didn't present any more than the usual problems. Then she must have seen another question coming up, so she said, firmly and finally: "It is a family matter. It has to be kept in the family, so we don't talk about it." End of quizzing. The comment struck me as rather strange, which is why I remember it.'

The professor finished his moment in the limelight with a grunt of self-satisfaction, and began jiggling his sherry glass. Kit saw a woman standing behind the drinks table grab a bottle and come over to fill the professor's glass. Kit recognised Katie Mc-Cullogh, who had done her doctorate under Genevieve some years ago.

'I asked you here to air your thoughts, not to take over the catering,' he whispered in her ear. He had told all those he had telephoned that he was anxious to find out who he was, and how he had come into the world and to Glasgow. He had prayed this declaration would turn out to be an attraction rather than an off-putter, and to his delight all who had said they could come had come.

'I'm happy to be barmaid,' whispered Katie back. 'If I don't talk I can listen, and so far I've heard pretty much all of the talk. It's been very interesting.'

'But you knew my mother better than most of the people here.'

'Maybe. But I only knew one side of her – the academic side. We talked about Caravaggio, not about little Kit. I don't remember her ever bringing up her personal life in conversation, and if I did it was carefully steered in another direction. I was never told anything of interest.'

They were interrupted by another man, a younger one, coming up to put in his penny-worth. He was fortyish, smart, perhaps even smarmy. At his approach Professor Pur-bright made an ambiguous noise and with-drew into the general throng.

'I say, I can vouch for what has been said about your father,' the newcomer said to Kit. 'He was discretion itself. These days we have started to think of newspapermen, even editors, as pushy people, discharging their personalities at you and all over you if you had the right sort of name or job.'

'That wasn't my father at all,' said Kit, thinking it might better describe the man who had just joined them.

'Oh,' said the man, a little deflated. 'I'd thought you might have more vivid memories of him than those of us who just met him on business or social occasions.'

'He really wanted to bring out my person-ality, not to parade his in front of me.'

'That's exactly it! So that's how he was with everyone, then. I saw him mostly in formal meetings, where nothing personal was called for, but I also met him at parties, receptions, that kind of thing. He didn't like mingling at large. He'd pick on someone, ask them what they did, then launch into questions about the job, ask about any new controversy about aspects of the job, what difference a Bill being pushed through Parliament would make. I know that was his technique because he used it on me, and I listened to him doing it to others.'

'What kind of people did he use it on?'

'Every kind! Politicians, churchmen, actresses, left-wing agitators. He got interesting things out of the least promising of individuals. It was almost as if he was a fiction writer, eager to extract possible ideas for novels.'

'Perhaps being deputy editor of a newspaper has some similarities to being a novelist. I don't mean that satirically, just that they extract gold from dross, interest from dreary reality. Glasgow's a very rich city in some ways.'

'That's true enough. I should know – I'm a solicitor, as perhaps you know.' (Paul Lawrence, then, whom Kit had asked because his mother often consulted him in the months of her illness.) 'People think Glasgow is all slums and Burrell Collections and the ice cream wars, but it's much richer than that.'

'What made you think of the ice cream wars?' Kit asked quickly.

'Because they have the true Glasgow spirit: violence, greed, but a touch of reality as well. Starts as an argument between ice cream sellers and their various patches, before long all hell breaks loose and the

Risorgimento is being fought all over again.' He thought for a moment. 'I suppose I mentioned the wars because I remember your father, a few years before he died, talking to someone at a conference about them. I mean, of course, about the gang warfare in general. People know by now that the ice cream wars were only a tiny section of the large picture – fights over territory, procedures, personal animosities.'

Kit stood uncertainly, sipping his sherry.

'I can't think, can't imagine, what connection there could be between my father, so gentle and scrupulous in his behaviour, and the Glasgow gangs. It wasn't a topic he talked about at home.'

'Perhaps any connection could have been professional rather than personal,' said Paul Lawrence, with his unendearing smirk.

'Meaning?'

'As a journalist he would have found the gangs good copy, and the ice cream wars were one of the things everybody knew about Glasgow without really understanding the details or the dynamics of the conflict.'

'I don't know... I wonder if there were ramifications in the ice cream wars that were personal to him.'

'You maybe have been unlucky in the timing of your father's death,' put in Professor Purbright, who had wandered around on the outskirts of the conversation.

'How's that?'

'Your father wouldn't have talked about any personal ramifications with any of the people here, because any connection with these people was pretty frail. The connection with your mother was probably the most important one in his life, and surely she must have known. The next most important connection was no doubt you. But how could he confide something possibly troubling to a young boy? He'd want you to be eighteen at least, probably more. I'm assuming what he had to confide, if he had anything, was somehow difficult, personal, embarrassing. How old were you when Jürgen died?'

'Seventeen.'

'And he'd been ill in hospitals and in a hospice for some time. I think you would have been told any secrets he might have had if only he'd lived a bit longer, and been in robust health.'

'I'm not sure my father was ever robust,' said Kit sadly.

'The thing everyone knows about your father was that he came to Britain with the train children – the Kindertransport,' said Paul Lawrence. 'That he didn't mind people knowing.'

'Well, there was nothing disgraceful or embarrassing about that,' said Kit stoutly.

'He felt that everyone concerned with it could be immensely proud of what they did. That we did talk about. He felt that so much credit was due to so many people and organisations that the best thing he could do for his adoptive country was to make his own rescue and survival as widely known as possible.'

'That sounds just like Jürgen,' said Purbright. But Kit turned back to Paul Lawrence.

'This conference or meeting or whatever it was where you listened to Jürgen talking to someone about gang warfare – what was it about? What body was it that my father belonged to? I ask because I met someone in Leeds who was an expert on gang culture in the major British cities. I just wondered–'

'Oh Lord,' said Lawrence, crinkling his brow. 'It was such a long time ago... I'm just trying to get a picture into my mind ... a picture of where we all were. That might tell me what we were at... No. Nothing's coming.'

'Was it St Andrews? The theological college?' It was Katie McCullogh, Kit's mother's PhD student of some years ago.

Lawrence swung round in her direction.

'The main hall, and the committee room beside it. You're quite right, it was there. Were you a delegate yourself?'

'No, but I was there – helping with the

refreshments. It was a conference bringing together–'

'All the racial and religious bodies in the big cities. It was one of these "We must encourage togetherness" do's. I always wonder whether we've got it right – whether friendly apartness isn't the best solution after all.'

'So what did this gang expert represent or talk about, then?' asked Kit.

'Oh, what the law can do to cut down on the beatings and the rivalry and the occasional slaughters – slaughters like that family here in Glasgow ... what was their name? Oh, the Doyles.' He looked at his watch. 'Oh Lord, I've got to go. I'm at the Theatre Royal tonight – the resuscitation of Scottish Opera.'

It was a signal to all of them to depart. Kit doubted if they all were going to Scottish Opera, but they clearly all felt they had done what little they could do to help Kit in his efforts – to do what they were not quite sure. Kit appealed to them to contact him if anything occurred to them – however trivial – and he distributed little cards he'd printed himself at Glasgow station with his mobile number on them. As they were making their farewells and voicing their good wishes Kit noticed that it was mostly the men who were going, and two of the women were holding back. He tried to speed up the departures without stinting on thanks and exhortations, and when they were all gone he turned back to the women.

'You wanted to talk to me,' he said. Katie McCullough nodded and introduced her friend, a stunning Scottish beauty of about her age.

'Yes, we wanted to talk. You'll have noticed there was a shortage of women here.'

'I was quite aware of that,' said Kit. 'I looked for more to invite, but couldn't find any among my mother's contacts. I also noticed a shortage of Scottish accents.'

'Pure south-east England most of them. We, the colonised, like to keep a low profile, particularly if there's any question of breaking confidence on things overheard while doing manual jobs for the university. Alison here, Alison McDermott, was another of your mother's doctoral students, both of us doing late sixteenth-century Italian paintings – Caravaggio and Moroni. It brought us together – also having your mother as supervisor.'

'I guess that means you were intrigued by her,' said Kit.

'Yes,' agreed Katie. 'Intrigued, fascinated, challenged. So we thought that any little thing might be of interest.' Kit nodded. 'Right. First, a date. You've been talking about an encounter between your father and a man who was closely involved with the "gang culture" of Glasgow – sorry about the awful phrase but it's one everybody uses. Anyway, Alison can tell you when that conference was.'

'We were both there,' said Alison, 'and we both saw it. It was the best view we'd had up to then of your father. I can date it because I only did waitressing jobs for one year of my doctorate, my second. So the encounter would have been between September 2002 and June 2003. That's for definite.'

'That's brilliant. You didn't know anything about the other man in the encounter?'

'No, except that he was probably involved in the law, since that was one of the main purposes of the conference.'

'Anything else?'

'Ye...e...es,' said Katie. 'This is not much more than an impression, but we'll give it to you for what it's worth. We saw a bit more than Mr Lawrence. He probably dashed off somewhere in a hurry – they say he's always doing that, and that it's a woman behind it rather than any of the good causes he names. So we saw this later on, during the lunch break. First we saw this unknown man edging towards Jürgen (we always called him that, though we didn't know him). He was edging towards his back, as if Jürgen might have avoided him if he'd seen him coming. We'd seen the man brushing off one or two people who'd tried to talk to him. Eventually the unknown man was standing just behind your father, waiting till

114

your father was finished with the person he was talking to. When he was, Jürgen turned around towards the buffet table where we were, so we saw everything that happened quite well. He saw Mr X waiting and he was very definitely not pleased.'

'I see,' said Kit, unsure what she had really observed in the incident. 'Now, why would this be? Had anything happened during the first encounter? Anything that maybe had angered or disgusted my father?'

'Not that we saw,' said Katie, 'but we were on duty: telling people what was in the pies, the quiches or whatever.'

'What more did you see?'

'Well,' said Alison, 'it was just a very tension-filled encounter. Your father, after the initial reaction, seemed to force his face to go blank. Like he was determined to give nothing away to any of the other people in the room. Neutral, unmoved, unexcited – that's how he tried to appear. But we both spotted the tenseness of the body, the strain between the two men, the feeling of an inactive volcano that was soon to explode. It was as if your father would have liked to resort to violence if he hadn't been, to the depths of his dearest convictions, one of those for whom violence never solved anything. I tell you, it was the most unusual episode I witnessed in the whole of my waitressing work that year.'

'In mine too,' said Katie.

'But some of the interest must have come from the fact that you were intrigued by my mother. Inevitably her marriage was up there among the most important aspects of her life and personality.'

'True,' admitted the women.

'Still, it's a very interesting encounter. Anything else?'

'Just a suggestion,' said Katie. 'About what you might do next.'

'Go on.'

'The thing everyone knows about your father is the Kindertransport.'

'As we were saying earlier.'

'Yes. There could be other things, things either connected to his Jewishness or to something quite different, that he would be less happy to have generally known. So he could have been using the rather heart-rending story about how he was saved from the gas chambers as a way of deflecting attention from something else. Sorry I can't put it in a more sensitive way.'

'I suppose I'd have to consider that. But it doesn't sound anything like my father.'

'Naturally you'd prefer the explanation you gave earlier – gratitude for his escape from death, and clear admiration for those who took part and risked death themselves. But we thought it might be worth going to talk to someone who really knows about the

116

Jewish-British relationship, and the Jewish-Continental relationship as well. I know a man who used to be leader of the Council for Jewish Studies, which is a misleading title: it's not an official body of any kind, just a talk shop, a group encouraging closer relationships and cooperation, and a sort of think tank illuminating dark areas in Jewish-British history. That means in particular what happened in the war.'

'What's this man's name?'

'Leo Kappstein. He's a retired academic – must be eighty-odd. Lives in Berwick-upon-Tweed, near where I come from: that's how I came to know about him. He was at one time into every controversy about Jewish history or about the Israeli government, which he fiercely defended, though he often in fact disapproved of what they were doing. He was one of the delegates at the conference we've been talking about.'

'He's still compos mentis?'

'Very much so.'

'Then I'll talk to him.'

'He'll be delighted. Like all old people he likes to be wanted, to be remembered.'

'I hope you're right. Depending on what information he has I might prove to be more an embarrassment than a pleasure.'

Kit was not to know that Leo Kappstein was to take his enquiries on to a whole new plane.

CHAPTER SEVEN

Secular Saint

The house that was home to Leo Kappstein seemed to Kit as he approached it to differ subtly from the other houses in Berwick-upon-Tweed. They, even the recent ones, seemed to be the product of border disputes in the distant past, not just facing north or south but anticipating trouble from one direction or the other. Leo Kappstein's was surrounded by a low wall, had a large 24 on the gate, and lawns that rolled down from what was nearly a bungalow to the road below, five minutes from the centre of the town.

Nearly a bungalow because what had once been one now had an extension on the back: a two-storey, multi-windowed small block which seemed designed to house records of some kind – files, reference books and newspapers, Kit guessed. It seemed that being keeper of the records was his host's life work.

His host had been watching for him. As he approached, the front door opened and a small man walked across the brilliant-green lawn to the front gate. How had he recognised him?

'I saw you once,' he said, leaning over the gate to shake Kit's hand, 'when I shared a taxi with your father, after one of our numerous meetings of worthy groups with excellent intentions. As we were dropping off Jürgen, you emerged from the front gate. I've trained myself to recognise and remember faces. You're known as Kit, I think...'

'That's right.'

'And I'm Leo Kappstein. I was so pleased when you rang asking to see me. Come through.'

As he opened the gate Kit realised that the house's doorbell was in fact a gatebell, and he guessed that the low wall was electronically primed to register any unauthorised intruders. Everything, he concluded, was geared to revealing callers wanted and unwanted to the sharp-eyed man of the house. There was here not quite a siege mentality, but close to it. Leo, a lean, fit-looking man in his seventies, saw that his caution had been noted.

'I get some funny visitors, usually unwanted,' he explained, as he led his guest up the lawn and towards the front door. 'Funny how the old style of nationalism is making such a strong revival, but it's done that every few years since the war. It's so easy to turn "peace" into a dirty word. I've always

119

believed that peace is the only answer.'

He ushered Kit into the bungalow and through into the front sitting room, where coffee and biscuits had already been laid out on the sideboard.

'I wrote to your mother when your father died, though I knew her only by his account of her. But I'd like to say to you now what I said to her. Your father was, in a quiet way, a great man. Nobody did more good and made less fuss about it. His was a difficult life, but he was a man of great humanity and even greater integrity, and his life was a beacon to others... There – I've said it now. Ask me whatever it is you think I can help you with. You're not Jewish by religion, I take it?'

There was a hungry, craving tone in his words, and behind them stood the shadow of the Holocaust.

'No, I'm not.'

'Pity. Pity to lose that. Still, still, I only ask because that is what a lot of people, especially people who got out of Germany just in time in the Thirties, come to me about. Wondering about what they've lost in the way of faith, and whether they should take it up again – if there was an "again" – or for the first time.' He chuckled. 'I always say they should try it. And I'd say the same to your generation, at one remove from the horrors of the Holocaust. Now, what is it that you're interested in?'

Kit had got his thoughts together on the train trip, but there was something that intrigued him in what Leo had just said.

'Before we get on to that, just one thing puzzles me. You said my father's was a difficult life. But he left Germany when he was three. I don't think of him as having a difficult life after that. Am I missing something somewhere? Is there something I haven't been told about?'

Leo Kappstein thought.

'No, it may not be a question of you having missed anything, or having had anything kept from you. You just see things differently from me. I see someone who, in leaving his country, lost also his religion. Most of the Jewish children who escaped to Britain were lodged with, and eventually adopted by, Jewish families. Jürgen and Hilde left at the height of the escaping fever, and there was no Jewish family to take care of or adopt them. Nothing was put in the way of the Philipsons, who were excellent people anxious to do good, but they were not Jews. They said they would ensure the two children had full knowledge of their background and religion, but I don't think their assurance amounted to much. I talked this over once with Hilde–'

'You knew Aunt Hilde?'

'I met her once – at a bar mitzvah.'

'It would be so much easier if she were still alive,' said Kit feelingly.

'I think it would,' agreed Leo, warmly. 'She had a sort of nostalgia for her old religion, but I got the impression that it was not strong enough for her to do anything decisive. So you see, I have my own viewpoint, and I think Jürgen often had difficulties and awful dilemmas, and I think that was mainly because, though he knew a little about Judaism, it was not a living force for him, and it would have been if things had been otherwise... And you mustn't forget Hilde. He grew up with her. She was only five years older than him, but during and after the escape from Germany she coped with all the everyday things quite brilliantly for a child of eight. You mustn't think I am blaming her because she couldn't cope with the larger things, but it was very natural that her mind concentrated on the immediate realities of the escape.'

'Yes, I do see, I think. Now if we could–'

'Come to the real reason why you are here. Yes, let's.'

'I think you know that I'm an adopted child.'

'Yes, I know that.'

'I learnt during my mother's last illness who my real family was. They were – they are – the family of a solicitor in Leeds. My adoptive mother was very cagey about the

122

"adoption"...' he sketched inverted commas with his hands, 'how it took place, and I began to suspect that no official adoption had taken place.'

'I see. So did you hear from your real mother and father, if they are still alive, how it had happened?'

'They are alive. No, I learnt most of the details before I came to know them. My mother called my birth family Novello, and said they were in her address book, and living in Leeds. More than that she would not say. I tried not to do anything before my mother died, because those months were for her and our time together. When she was dead I knew what I needed to do. I knew exactly when they had received me after my so-called adoption because that was always kept as a special day – a day to be celebrated. Fortunately it was in the school holidays – August the twentieth. I had in my mind some very vague memories of an early childhood home, other parents. I went to the newspapers in the Glasgow University library and found little references to my birth parents in the national papers, and even briefer ones in the Scottish papers...'

'And?'

'I found that the name Novello, which my mother had told me was my birth name, was also the name of an English child who had been abducted in Sicily.'

Leo Kappstein frowned, and only after a minute asked: 'If you were abducted, why was there so little press interest?'

Kit shook his head.

'I don't know. It seems the police here thought it was an Italian matter – and they left it to the Italian police. Or maybe whoever organised the kidnapping had some kind of heft in the newspaper world. Or else only the most sensational cases get mass-media coverage. I believe there are thousands of abductions a year in this country alone, and very few get more than mine got. Most get none at all.'

'And the Madeleine McCann case?'

'She had a beautiful mother, professional parents – people who could be built up and then knocked down, which the press loves to do. And of course, they themselves thought publicity was vital, to make sure the general public was on the alert to look out for her.'

'That makes sense,' admitted Leo. 'Italy, you say?'

'Yes. Do you see any special significance in that?'

'I don't know. The fact that you were kidnapped there must surely give it some significance. Questions arise, don't they?'

'Such as?'

'Were you kidnapped because you were ... what was your birth name?'

'Peter Novello.'

'Ah, yes... Or were you just kidnapped because your family was on holiday, seemed to have the sort of money needed to pay a ransom, and so on?'

'Except that no ransom was ever demanded.'

'Really?'

'Not so far as I can discover. Which suggests, rather, that I was abducted because I was Peter Novello.'

'An Italian surname. Perhaps some kind of revenge on your father, or on some other family member?'

'I have problems with my birth father. Let's come back to him later. Any other significance of Italy?'

Leo Kappstein shrugged.

'The fate of Italian Jews under Mussolini is a topic that engages many people today. I have been interested in it since I started my work, more than fifty years ago. My work is both for reconciliation between warring parties and also to help and identify survivors of the Holocaust – Jewish survivors, homosexual survivors, Gypsy survivors ... and also Nazi survivors. Some people have tried to make Mussolini out to be a benign figure so far as the Jews were concerned. But he was just a less obsessed, and less efficient, Hitler.'

'Can this have any relevance to me, and

who I am? Even my father – he never did more than say he was a Jew. I don't think it meant much more to him than just a simple fact.'

Kappstein looked at him.

'And yet I'd wager he thought about that simple fact every day of his life.'

Kit felt himself rebuked.

'He talked a lot about the "Kindertransport". I'm sure that stayed with him,' Kit said.

'Did he talk about his family?'

'Hilda, of course. Excuse the pronunciation. That's how I always knew and thought of her – as an English woman. She was a regular visitor to us right up to her death. Otherwise... I do remember him once saying something that suggested that his father was still alive. That puzzled me, because he obviously was not talking about Grandad Philipson. If Jürgen's real father in Germany was alive, why did we never see him, get letters from him, talk about him?'

'Didn't you ask your father about him?'

'I thought about it at the time. I nearly did. But I saw that my father had noticed that I'd heard his words and been puzzled. He cleared his throat and turned away and ... I can't explain it.'

'I think I understand, though,' said Leo. 'He was a man of quietness, of very restrained gestures. You, as one very close to him, would know when he wanted to keep silent on a topic.'

'Yes, that's it,' said Kit. 'That's exactly it. He was so reserved that you always thought twice before trying to draw him out. By and large he preferred not to make difficult things explicit.'

'But he could talk about the rescue of children like himself, you say?'

'Yes. But that was something he could be entirely and utterly positive about. And grateful. Britain was a country – still, he would always emphasise – where there was a sizeable minority who would ensure that the moral side to every question was thoroughly debated. Imagine the Germans in the Thirties debating the moral side of killing the Jews! But the situation of the Jews had to be debated in Britain, in the most practical way possible, by extending the hand of hospitality.'

'However reluctantly at times,' put in Leo. 'But I must not be mean-minded. You are quite right. Britain's action was a contribution to a moral debate that almost everyone else sidestepped.'

'What worries me,' said Kit, 'is connections.'

'What connections are they?'

'That's what I'd like to know. I'm worried about the lack of connections. I am told by my adoptive mother that my real mother is

127

a Mrs Novello, of Leeds. I accept that because I retain faint memories of Isla and her house, particularly my old bedroom. But what is the connection between a Leeds solicitor's family and a literary/academic family in Glasgow headed by a Jewish refugee?'

'Perhaps the kidnap was the work of one of the Glasgow gangs,' suggested Leo. 'Plenty of Italian – especially Sicilian – elements there. Though why you should be kidnapped to order is beyond me. But then, perhaps you weren't. Coincidences happen. Tell me, what does it say on your birth certificate?'

'Just "adopted". I thought the certificate would be useful, but then, of course, it couldn't say the mother's name because many prefer to keep it from the child.'

'And of course, the certificate could be a forgery. That is one of the things that Glasgow crooks do very well. Passports, marriage certificates, nationalisation papers – you want it, they can do it. For a price.'

'Yes, of course. It's quite possible that the only genuine birth certificate I'll ever have will be as Peter Novello. Isla is sure to have one.'

'Would that worry you?'

'It would a bit. I loved Jürgen and Genevieve. They were my loving parents from the age of three. I felt at ease, comfortable, confident with them. I can imagine, with time, feeling the same about Isla. But the fact will remain that I grew up with the Philipsons, went through all the pleasures and pains of childhood and adolescence with them. My personal papers ought to record that in some way.'

'I can understand that,' said Leo. 'For me you are – let's say – not a part of Jürgen's family, because you are not Jewish. But of course, Jürgen had married outside his religion, and apparently never practised the faith after he left Germany. He and Genevieve ought to be awarded the lion's share of the credit for your upbringing.'

Kit decided to change the subject a shade.

'Tell me, I'm told you were at a meeting which I suspect both my birth father and my adopted father attended.'

'Really? It's perfectly possible. I am an inveterate attender of meetings, because I have to be buoyed up with optimism, with a feeling of doing something. What was the meeting about?'

'About bringing down barriers among peoples, races, groups. It was held at the St Andrew's Theological College in Glasgow in about 2002. But what I'm interested in is what happened between the two men.'

'They met? Talked?'

'Yes. I gather my Leeds birth father was prominent in peace talks among the various

Glasgow gangs – the ice cream wars and so on. Often there would be a wholly or partially Italian component to these groups, and their disagreements were most often about territories: which should be serviced by which ice cream vendor. Sounds absurd, but that was the truth of it. That's how they began, though they burgeoned into something much bigger. A British legal man with Italian as one of his languages could be very useful when peace talks had been arranged.'

'Yes – and you're saying he could have got closer to some of the big names in the gangs than he ought to have done?'

'Yes. Perhaps he was compromised in some way, and was forced into things he detested. Perhaps he simply used the gangs himself, having acquired a lot of influence through his apparently above-board work negotiating and peacemaking. It's a mystery, but one we have a chance of solving as he's still alive. The only point I'm making is that he is very likely a link.'

'And did something happen at this meeting I was apparently at that illustrated his connection with the gangs?'

'Not quite that. But it suggested some connection between my birth father and Jürgen. They talked in the coffee break of this meeting–'

'At such meetings everybody talks.'

'Yes, but something must have been said

that angered my ... angered Jürgen. I think my birth father approached Jürgen for a second time that day in the lunch break and for once my father couldn't hide his emotions. When he saw who was about to accost him again, I'm told his face showed absolute detestation, and he turned away – frozen-faced again – to avoid my father and any further contact between them.'

'I see,' said Leo thoughtfully. 'Could it be that it was at this time that Jürgen learnt who you actually were?'

'I suppose it's possible. There's a slightly dog-eared note under the name Novello in Jürgen's address book – "Kit's mother" is all it says – enough, I suppose, but no date is given.'

'Tell me,' said Kappstein, 'what you know about Jürgen's birth father and mother.'

Kit raised his eyebrows in surprise.

'Very little. His mother died, it's thought, in Auschwitz or perhaps Dachau. His father, I believe – I don't know – was still alive seven or eight years ago, though if so he must have been very old. Maybe bed-ridden or mentally disturbed and unable to travel. I am guessing here, of course. All I have to go on are those few words, which I don't actually remember, of my father's. Something like, "I ought to go and see him." Or maybe, "I'd like to go and see him."'

'Yes ... I feel most at home with the Jewish

side of your parentage, though I understand a fair bit of Scottish mores and opinions by now, and even Italians sometimes have revealed their mysteries to me. But I can try to find in the archives anything I may have on your father's birth family.'

'Yes please. I suppose you don't know his name...'

'Oh, but I do. Your father was a Horovitz, and at the time of his birth his father was known as Samuel Horovitz and his mother as Lisabeth. Apart from the genuine name, your grandfather called himself all sorts of things, Greenspan among them – I found it quite bewildering, but I'll find my way around his various personae eventually. I've made a start. I took the trouble to look up your father after I had your phone call last night which arranged this meeting. Until I lose my marbles you will find me quite boringly well organised and terribly well informed.'

'Do you know what happened to my grandfather?'

'He was not one of nature's victims. There were a lot of rumours, but no rumour of his being in one of the German camps.'

'What did the rumours concern?'

'East European countries mostly. Hungary, Romania, for example. Both places where Jews were persecuted – had been for centuries – but the persecution intensified when the political leaders of the countries became Fascists. But the most frequent place of refuge and the subject of most rumours about your grandfather was Italy.'

'That surprises me,' said Kit, shifting uneasily in his chair. 'Mussolini was Hitler's henchman, surely. Fleeing to Italy would be going from the frying pan into the fire.' Kappstein shook his head.

'Not quite. Mussolini was Hitler's ally, several steps down as a Fascist leader of importance. This riled him. He had a ten-year lead in the catalogue of Fascist countries; he'd given the world the word and many of the ideas – that's what the poor man thought – he was Europe's inspiration. It's often said he was lukewarm in the persecution of the Jews. There's some truth in that, but it was not a matter of conscience or tender-heartedness. He just saw it as one of Hitler's pointless obsessions. He thought it was better to screw money out of them.'

'What changed his mind?'

'The course of the war. By the time of the Allied invasion of Italy in 1943 he had no future except tied to Hitler's chariot wheels, and he soon realised that wholesale spoliation of the Italian Jews' fortunes was a wonderful source of revenue, and he began that with energy and efficiency.'

'Right,' said Kit slowly. 'So if my grandfather didn't land up in the German camps he could have died in their Italian equivalents.'

'Possible. But far fewer of the Italian Jews died. And if we are right about his activities, they were always on the windy side of the law. If he was in Italy, if he was incarcerated there, what should such a man have done?'

Kit thought.

'Teamed up with his Italian equivalents? The Mafia, the Camorra, all sorts of small and large gangsters.'

'Yes, exactly. And rumour has him in a camp called Ferramonti in the Kingdom of the Two Sicilies – the old kingdom centred on Naples, and including Sicily and the bottom of mainland Italy, the part of Italy that was liberated fairly early by the Allies.'

'This does begin to sound promising.'

'But remember to be careful. This is almost conjecture, supported only by rumour. Courage and caution, that's what you must show. I want to help you, and I will do, so long as I am mentally active. Remember, a lot of my information is inconvenient to the people who consult me. For example, your grandfather used a series of different names – practically a new name every time he went to a new city. Up to no good? Probably. The name he bequeathed to his children was Greenspan, but as I have discovered, that was not his real or legal name.'

'I'll remember that.'

'Good. Being a pedant, even about births and deaths rather than grammar, is a very inconvenient thing. But it may prevent you going off into cul-de-sacs, that I can promise you.'

But, leaving the bungalow in the afternoon sunlight, Kit felt torn between contrary emotions. He had liked Leo Kappstein. On the other hand he had a niggling sense that the man was holding back on something, perhaps even playing with him. And he had been shocked by Leo's admission that for him he, Kit, a non-Jew, was not part of Jürgen's 'family'. He was quite sure Jürgen had not felt the same. But then he was of another generation.

And what was it that had really made his father's life 'difficult'?

CHAPTER EIGHT

Undercurrents

'Peter!' said Isla, when she opened her front door to her son two days later.

'Isla!' said Kit. They embraced, but the two words left a legacy of embarrassment which it took some time to dispel. Isla looked at the two smallish suitcases her son was carrying and definitely had to smother feelings of disappointment.

'Oh good, you've brought some of your things,' she said.

'Just a few,' said Kit. 'So that I have two sets of the important things when I'm here.'

'Yes ... I've had a second set of keys made for you,' said Isla, but carefully, as if she knew she was on delicate terrain. Kit responded a shade too enthusiastically.

'Great! Though I'm not sure I ought to treat this house as my own, barging in whenever I feel like it.'

'You barge in, Kit. You can't interrupt any-thing important, or anything I'd blush to have you see for that matter. Now, you go up and unpack your things and we'll have a nice drink before dinner. Gin and tonic suit you?'

'Fine.'

'And I've got pork fillet for dinner.' She noticed or imagined that a shadow passed over his face as she spoke. 'Oh dear! Have I done something silly?'

'No, not at all. I eat pork, ham and all that stuff – always have. My mother wasn't Jewish, as you know, and Dad was a sort of halfway Jew. That meant we didn't have it that often for dinner, so it's a sort of treat. Pork fillet will be fine.'

And certainly when he came to eat it Isla could detect no sign of nausea or hesitation. Before that, over the gin and tonics with the obligatory lemon, Isla asked how things had gone in Glasgow.

'Fine. I got things done in connection with my mother's will – things that needed sorting out.' On an impulse he ventured on a half-truth. 'And I heard one or two things about my father that I want to look into.'

'Which father?'

Looking quickly up and then down Kit saw that Isla's face was flushed a blood-red.

'Jürgen Philipson. It was just an incident, something that happened at one of those do-gooding conferences he was often a delegate at. I've learnt that he made it clear, without a word spoken, that he had the strongest objections to another of the delegates. The whole encounter was so unlike my father's usual self that it made me think. Why would

137

he have been so upset? I'm going to try to find out who that other person was, and if he could have had anything to do with my "adoption".'

'Isn't that a terribly long shot? Why should your father have anything against someone who helped him to get you? I should have thought he'd be eternally grateful.'

She was now her usual colour. Kit looked straight into her eyes.

'I don't know about you, but it seems to me that a good man – as my father was – would be the last person on earth who would want to benefit from a child abduction.'

Isla swallowed.

'Yes, of course. If he knew–'

'There are all sorts of possibilities: for example, that he did not know how I'd been taken from my birth parents, but he found out from the man he immediately took an aversion to. By that time, by the way, I must have been about fifteen, so it would have been a bit of an academic question: they'd surely never have taken me away from my adoptive parents?'

'Who wouldn't?'

That pulled Kit up in his tracks.

'Well, I suppose I mean the police – or the authorities generally. Oddly enough I really know very little about adoption. And the abduction would still have been a police

138

matter, even though it happened a long time before and the British police had always left matters to the Italian police. By the time they'd got anywhere, if they ever did, I'd have been practically of legal age for sure.'

Later, when they were eating apple crumble, Isla said: 'I wish I understood why you're doing all this rummaging about in the past. What good is it going to do? Why can't you just accept the facts: you were stolen from me, and landed up somehow as the adopted child of people you liked and respected. Not a too dreadful fate, was it?'

'No, of course not... Remember, Isla, that the first step in this "rummaging" – I'd prefer to call it amateur detective work – was finding you. As soon as I knew that Genevieve was not my birth mother, finding you became my aim: to find my real mother and to know who I was, and how it happened. And to try to lessen the pain you must have felt at losing your young child.'

'I realise that, and I'm glad and grateful.'

'And I found out how it was done, the abduction, and I'm glad to know. But the question arises: how did I come to belong to Jürgen and Genevieve? How would they connect with Sicilian kidnappers? How did I get from Sicily to Glasgow?

'Of course, I don't know,' said Isla, now more subdued. 'Till you turned up I had no idea where you were or who you were with.'

'No, you didn't – couldn't have. Even after they knew about your identity, or began to have suspicions, Jürgen and Genevieve couldn't have made contact with you, for fear of losing me. And, of course, I understand that it's not as important to you to know the details as it is to me. I want to know to fill in gaps in my knowledge of the past, but also to understand the psychology of what happened. How did two high-minded, law-abiding citizens come to acquire a child in so dubious a way? How did they come to profit by a crime they would have abhorred?'

'It's a mystery,' said Isla, now almost complacent. 'But I don't see that you had anything to do with it. You were too young. Isn't it time you got on with your life and stopped worrying about what happened in the past and why? I know that's what I would do.'

'Well, maybe that's what I will be forced to do if I get nowhere. But it's definitely second best. I know I won't feel happy and complete unless I've tried to make sense of it all.'

Isla shook her head.

'Well, I'll hold my peace. You're not going to take advice from a silly old woman, I realise that.'

Kit shook his head and grinned.

'You don't regard yourself as silly, Isla, and

140

I'm pretty sure you don't see yourself as old either.' They both laughed. 'And neither do I.'

As they were preparing for bed Isla tentatively asked Kit what he was going to do the next day.

'I thought of driving into Leeds,' he said. 'They say it's very hard to find your way around, so I thought I'd make a start.'

'Oh, that's a good idea. You can take my car.'

'But I don't need to. I have my car. I drove down.'

Isla left a pause, obviously not trusting herself to speak. It was clear that Kit's paucity of luggage was doubly painful to her if he had had a car to load it into.

'Of course. You'd have inherited the Philipsons' car, wouldn't you?'

'Yes. We sold Jürgen's soon after he died. Genevieve's is the car I learnt to drive in. I drove it a lot in the last few months of her life, when we were going to all her favourite places. Is there anything I can do for you tomorrow in Leeds?'

'Oh no, I don't think so,' said Isla, still sounding a bit miffed.

However, by the next day she had changed her mind, and had a job for him.

'I've got this cake I made and iced for the Leeds Ladies' Guild. It's our fiftieth anniversary. Formed when dear old Harold

Macmillan was prime minister by Leeds ladies who thought the Women's Institutes weren't good enough for them. We're all baking something and Ada Micklejohn said she'd take it for me because I can't go. Well, won't, more like. I don't go along much these days. It was my excrement of a husband who persuaded me to join, but I never felt at home with the Leeds Ladies – not my style at all. Ada lives in The Calls. I'll give you a map. And you must let her show you her books.'

'Her books? Is she a collector? Or an academic?'

'The first if anything,' said Isla, hardly bothering to hide an overtone of contempt. 'Be respectful. And don't say rude things about Barbara Cartland.'

'Why on earth would I say rude things about Barbara Cartland? I barely know who she was.'

'And don't say that either.'

Kit, with the aid of Isla's map and rather more aid from his *A to Z* street directory, found The Calls without difficulty, and a parking space through divine intervention. He spoke his identity ('I'm Isla's son') into the list of tenants on the door and was rewarded by a 'Oh, do come up. The door's open. It's the cake isn't it? He pushed open the street door and by following directions found his way to flat 237, Ada's home.

When he rang the bell the door was opened immediately and Ada Micklejohn appeared, apparently already in full flood. Kit had a vision of shiny silk drapes and caked make-up while the melting-chocolate voice flowed into one ear and out the other.

'I got in right at the beginning here in The Calls, and this flat is one of the biggest, and I didn't pay a fortune for it, far from it, but I've always had an eye for a bargain, that's what you need these days, lovely that Isla has you back, how were things wherever it was you've been? No don't tell me, my travelling days are over, did Isla tell you I've got two flats here? I snapped up the one next door the moment it came on the market, here – just have a look because you're sure to sneer, now don't say you won't because I know you will, know by experience, particularly young men, but here we are, three rooms with nothing but my collection...' She threw open the door and Kit was greeted by a room totally devoted to books, climbing to the ceiling, supplemented by free-standing bookcases and boxes containing as yet un-classified items to be shelved later.

'Ah,' he said, remembering Isla's words, 'a library of romantic fiction.'

'Not of romantic fiction generally, that's beyond my scope, no, this, young fellow, is the world's largest collection of Mills & Boon, with only a hundred and fifty-seven titles yet to be found. I've got people scouring the world, devoted lovers of really good writing, and what a collection of happiness after misery along the way the whole collection will represent, and so much learning, remember dear Barbara Cartland saying, "I was trained as a historian", and what knowledge she put into her historicals! I worship her, and always so tastefully presented' – she threw a hand in the direction of the collection, with many volumes facing outwards to display the execrable artwork that would certainly have had Genevieve Philipson either shuddering or laughing.

'I'm not sure I could take all those happy endings,' said Kit. 'My mother once said there was nothing so depressing as a happy ending. You think of all the disillusionment in store for the couple.'

'Don't you believe your crabby mother,' said Ada, and Kit carefully restrained himself from correcting her on which mother he had been talking about. 'She's a particular case, and I've nothing to say to excuse your father, that's for sure, but your mother had her revenge, and she had a lot of happiness over the years from you children that's for sure, and I know how happy you've made her, how she's revelled in your success, are you going to marry that girl of yours, do you think she's worthy of you? Your mother doesn't, I'm sure you know that, but what mother ever does? Eh? I think she'll be over the moon to have you back, put the cake down there, will you?' They had come into the main flat, which was decorated in Regency style with – again, and most unfortunately – the originals of Mills & Boon covers ruining the atmosphere on the walls. 'You won't have a cup of tea, will you, or something stronger? No, I can see it in your face, you won't go and see your father, will you? I know Micky does – Micky's the only one of you I've met – I don't know why he should, or you either, or the other one whose name I forget, you owe him nothing, that's for sure, and when they separated your mother had all the burden and he barely acknowledged his family's existence, not just the one but all of you, I know that because Isla told me herself, now you will come again, won't you, there's so much I can show you.'

'I will, I will,' said Kit, not altogether untruthfully, disappearing down the corridors. In fact, he had been disappearing out the door when the full significance of what Ada was saying – of everything Ada had said – was brought home to him. Kit slowed down, let himself thoughtfully out of the maze of flats, and went and sat in his car, wondering what to do next.

He had passed by the police headquarters in the city on his search to find a parking space. He felt pretty sure it was not far away. After weighing up the pros and cons he left the car where it was, locating the station by its closeness to the bus terminal. When he went up to the desk to ask for Sergeant Hargreaves the desk man was on the blower to him in a trice. The looming, going-to-seed figure of the sergeant appeared promptly, and led Kit off to find one of the interview rooms.

'I can see something has happened,' said Hargreaves. 'I can see it in your face.'

'Not exactly happened,' said Kit. 'But I think I may have made a discovery. Whether it's important or not I don't think I'm the best one to judge.'

'Spill the beans.'

Kit told him the gist of the meeting, cutting down on Ada's devotion to romantic fiction. ('My wife reads Mills & Boon,' said the sergeant. 'Women's rubbish. She says they show her what she's been missing all these years.') When he finished Hargreaves stretched his legs in the chair.

'Well!' he said.

'Yes. When we talked about Isla having me back I thought she'd been told about my reappearance by Isla. But then she talked about my "success" and my girlfriend (I haven't got one at the moment that Isla knows about). I was just going out the door when I realised she was confusing me with

146

Dan. It could be useful in the future if that's what she thinks. She might talk about "Peter", as they call me, more openly, without inhibitions. Whether that would actually be useful is another matter. The confusion of the two sons is symptomatic of a general confusion in Ada's mind, which probably Isla doesn't understand or at least take any notice of. One tends to switch off in the general flood of talk, going from subject to subject. For example, what do you make of what she said about my father?'

Hargreaves stretched again, and thought hard before he replied.

'First of all, he's done something that Isla condemns. We must be careful, Isla is far from being an unbiased witness.'

'Agreed.'

'Still, I compared it in my mind with your encounter with your father, which you wrote me a nice full account of. Do you see what I'm getting at?'

'I think so.'

'He refused to acknowledge you. That could mean at least two things. One is that he doesn't think you are the three-year-old son that was abducted.'

'Yes. Though if so he never spelt it out.'

'Secondly, it could mean that he never acknowledged that that member of the family was his child. You're "not any kind of son" was how he put it. That's pretty comprehensive, isn't it? What he may have been saying is that you were Isla's son, but not by him. Maybe that he tried to make the situation work back in your early childhood, but found he never could accept you.'

'Yes. I haven't had much time to think that over, but that was one of the possibilities that occurred to me. It makes one feel a bit more sympathetic to the man.'

'It makes you feel that way. But you're a nice lad and you try to make the best of people, no doubt as you were taught to do by your also nice parents. But would you say that the rest of the interview you had with your father suggested he was the sort of man who would try to make the best of a situation like that for the sake of his wife, and to keep the family together?'

Kit thought hard.

'No... But of course, this is twenty years after the event. He could have changed.'

'Have you heard anything about how he treated his acknowledged family after the separation or divorce?'

'Divorce. He paid very little attention to them.'

'That seems to chime in with the impression he made on you.'

'Yes.'

'Did he virtually cast them off right from the time of the split-up?'

'Not quite, but not long afterwards.'

148

'And they are his real children – no question about that. Since you've come back I suppose that's what you've naturally assumed yourself to be too. Legally it's what you are. But if Novello wiped his own children out of his life, how much more is he likely to want to wipe you out of the historical record if he believes, rightly or wrongly, that you're not his? And there's another thing–'

'If I'm not his, whose am I?' said Kit.

'Spot on. And is the identity of your father an added grievance that made it even more impossible for Frank Novello to form any bond with you?'

Kit held up his hand, palm outward.

'Wait. Let's not go further.'

'You've got to face facts, lad.'

'Facts yes. But we're not at the moment in the realm of facts, but in the realm of conjecture. If we're going to stay in the realm of conjecture we ought to sit down and examine some of the other possible conjectures.'

'Like?'

'That I was his favourite son, and the marriage collapsed after he lost me.'

Hargreaves considered this.

'Possible. I'd have expected a lawyer to make a tremendous fuss if he lost his own child in a kidnap.'

'Fuss with whom? Police? Press?'

'Either. Both probably, and politicians as well, but principally police. I don't get any sense from the records that he did anything much other than keep in touch through the British police with what was going on in Sicily.'

'Where the police were doing bugger all.'

'Exactly.'

'The question is, what do I do next?'

'Yes... I'd say you've got to face up to your father's part in all this. Not by talking to him again, because you'd most likely get exactly the same result: stonewalling and sadistic games.'

'Sadistic games,' mused Kit. 'I sometimes wonder whether the whole abduction wasn't part of a sadistic game.'

'Good point. At the expense of your birth mother, perhaps. Perhaps one should say that the whole business has Frank Novello's thumbprint on it.'

'I could talk to Micky,' said Kit. 'He needs to think a bit more about his father, to think what in general makes Frank tick. Did the family ever notice – the younger ones – any aversion to me as a child? I ought to try to get him to be honest, to really examine his memories.'

'And there's one more person you have to talk to,' said Hargreaves.

'Who's that?'

'Isla Novello. She knows most of all. Perhaps she knows everything. You have to get her to be honest too. She lost a child. Why didn't she react more strongly at the time?'

Kit groaned. It was something he had known since his return, and had tried not to face up to.

'We've tried,' he said, then amended it to: 'We've skirted the surface.'

'But even if you learn all she knows,' said Hargreaves, ever the practical man in the street, 'you'll still be only through the first stage, and have hardly dipped a toe into the second.'

'Which is?'

'How you came to land up in Glasgow, Scotland, as the child of Jürgen and Genevieve Philipson.'

CHAPTER NINE

Another Sort of Family Reunion

The voice came down the telephone: 'Mother?'

Kit was standing beside Isla at the phone, where they had been discussing what he would like for dinner. He recognised the voice as that of Micky's wife, Pat, but he recalled her at the party as always referring to Isla as 'Mum'. The tone of voice and the more formal word made him wonder if a new ice age was in preparation.

'Yes, Pat. Who else?'

'Mother, what is this about Kit being–?'

'Kit is standing beside me, Pat.' Isla said this in her most schoolmistressy voice. She did not mention the fact that he had immediately moved away. There was a nonplussed silence at the other end.

'Well, I've nothing against Kit. Nothing at all. It's just that–'

'That what?'

Another silence.

'We're coming round.' The tone of determination suggested that Pat was proposing a family excursion to the South Pole. 'The children will have to come, but they can play in the garden,' she went on.

'That's as you please, Pat. Kit and I will make sure that we're here.'

'I have some phone calls to make. We'll be there in twenty minutes.'

'Hmmm,' said Isla, putting the phone down. 'She's a troublemaker, that one, and trouble is what we'll have.'

When the twenty-minute deadline loomed Kit retreated to the dining room and watched the street outside. Micky Novello drove a three-year-old Honda Civic and when it stopped outside the front gate five people scrambled out of it, Micky looking very troubled. They were received at the front door by Isla and were still bundling the children out into the back garden and keeping them quiet with sweets and pop when another car drew up – a car verging on limousine status, though Kit didn't recognise the make or model, out of which got his sister Maria and her husband Ivor Battersby. Ivor spotted Kit in the window and raised his hand, and Kit was about to reciprocate friendship in kind (he might need all the friendship he could get) by going out into the melee when yet another car drew up. It said Stanningley Cars on the roof and side, and out of it got the determined but slightly comic figure of Wendy Maclean, and following her – yes, it had to be – his younger brother Dan: smart, be-suited, his hair glued up in rough spikes that resembled a rampant bramble growing on moorland. He looked the epitome of a promising footballer up on a charge of rape, affray or dangerous driving.

Kit, without wanting to, felt he had to go out and join the party. The introduction to Dan was as brief and formalised as it could be, and the whole party then gathered in the Seldon Road dining room.

'What we want to know,' said Pat, gazing round at what she obviously regarded with satisfaction as a full house, 'is how come we've never been told? How come Isla hasn't made it clear that the kid who was abducted in Sicily had a different father to the rest of her children, and was in fact illegitimate? Why were we left in the dark?'

There was a single voice that shouted 'Hear! Hear!' – at first loudly, but fading away.

A long silence followed.

'I never told anyone because it's not true,' Isla finally said, quietly. Kit thought with amused approval that Isla was likely to play her hand much more effectively than Pat. He thought, also, that he knew exactly where Pat had obtained her information.

'You introduced Kit to the family as one of us, and the next stage would have been that he came in for his quarter of the family estate,' Pat said.

'He can still do that,' said Isla, her chin going up a degree or two. 'There is no "family" estate. My house and my money are mine to do what I like with – mine absolutely. Unfortunately, Kit rejects the whole idea of inheriting his share from me.'

'I came in for a house and sufficient money from my adoptive parents,' said Kit, keeping his voice low. 'That is more than enough for me.'

'Pull the other one,' said Pat, her tone becoming broader Yorkshire and harsher as she felt more floundering than victorious. 'When is money ever enough? And I never heard that you were adopted by billionaires.'

'I don't suppose you know anything about my parents,' said Kit, voice still soft and impersonal.

'This is really very distasteful,' said Ivor Battersby suddenly. 'And futile. Isla leaves her estate as she likes, and if Kit gives his share to Christian Aid or the Dogs Trust, that's a matter entirely for him. Bringing it up like this is not only distasteful, it's shabby.'

'Who the hell are you to criticise?' said Dan, an unlovely sneer on his face. 'You're not family. It's we who've had someone foisted on us who turns out to have been born on the wrong side of the blanket.'

'I doubt whether you would know which

155

was the wrong and which was the right side,' said Ivor contemptuously. 'I can't take a footballer's moral outrage seriously.'

'Dan,' said Isla. 'I have no idea when you came back from Australia, or why you didn't tell me when you were coming or had come, but you'd be well advised to hold your peace and not mess with things that are well beyond your comprehension and have nothing to do with you.'

'It's an outrage – having a cuckoo foisted on us who immediately lines up for his share of the family loot,' said Dan.

'I seem to have been misunderstood,' said Kit, trying hard not to treat Dan with disdain but not succeeding. 'I wanted to make it clear that I was not lining up to receive Novello family money or possessions.'

'I've been trying to think,' said Isla, in a meditative voice, 'where all this innuendo could have come from. There is only one source I could think of.' She shut her mouth determinedly and looked straight at Micky. He held her gaze for a few seconds, and then looked down.

'Anyway, what does it matter?' asked Ivor Battersby. 'You're not a titled family. And if you were, what difference would that make? There's hardly a person in the world can be one hundred per cent sure who their father is, and that includes the aristocracy.'

'That's what I'm trying to say,' said Isla.

'Thank you, Ivor. Kit is of the right blood group. He was born to me, and into what seemed to be a stable marriage. One more child was born after him. My husband, all the time of the separation and divorce, never once made any allegation that he was not the father of Peter Novello. What more do you want?'

'In any case, it's irrelevant,' said Maria.

'Of course it is,' said Isla. 'Ivor was right. In the olden days women went with so many lovers that every child could have had a different father. There was a Duchess of Devonshire like that – long, long ago, of course. And there was Winston Churchill's mother – she had a string of men. Nobody went up to Winston and said "We'd like you to take a blood test before we let you save the nation". All this "illegitimate" and "legitimate" hardly matters to anyone these days.'

'It matters to me,' said Dan, who had no sense of the ridiculous. 'When you go I shall expect to get my third of the estate.'

Everyone looked at Isla.

'You were always my favourite child,' she said.

'I know, Ma,' whined Dan. 'So why are you doing this to me?'

'I think in the future I shall show less favouritism. In fact, at this moment it would give me great satisfaction to leave you nothing at all.'

'Mum!' wailed Dan.

'Can I just have a word?' asked Kit. 'I seem to be in the middle of a discussion which is all about me, but I don't have anything to contribute to it.'

'Then pipe down,' said Dan.

Kit ignored him.

'First I'd like to guess that the person who raised the question of paternity was the man I thought, since coming here, was generally agreed to be my father. I'm guessing that Micky paid him one of his regular visits and got landed with this confidence. Is that right, Micky?'

Micky nodded miserably.

'Yes. Yes, it was him who told me. I shouldn't have passed it on. I'm sorry.'

He spoke in an undignified mumble, close to tears.

'You'd have been in dire trouble if you hadn't passed it on,' said Pat.

'And did he reveal the name of anyone whom he guessed, or had evidence about, who might be my biological father?'

'We'll talk afterwards, Kit,' said Micky.

'All right – that's good enough. But then there's the question of the abduction. Did he say anything about that?'

'Not much. Said he never could accept you – hated to be near you. When he told me that, little scraps of memory came back to me: of his never playing with you, hardly even talking to you.'

'Shame on him,' said Isla.

'Anyway, he said that in the end the kidnapping solved his problem.'

There was silence, everybody thinking of the implications of the words.

'He didn't say he arranged the abduction, to solve the problem?' Kit asked.

'No.'

'But that possibility is one that he left open?'

'I suppose so. I just took it to mean that it was a coincidence but, still, it did solve the problem.'

'Except that soon after Dan's birth Dad moved out of the family home and the marriage was over,' said Maria. 'That could have solved the problem without anything as sensational as an abduction. I remember that, young as I was. It was a horrible time.'

'Where does all that leave us?' asked Pat Novello, nagging away at the bone of her grievance. 'We should be clear about that.'

'It leaves Micky, Maria and Dan set to inherit one third each of the estate that I will leave since Kit has disclaimed his rightful share,' said Isla. She looked around and saw a degree of relaxation in the shoulders of the two men. 'Of course, I have a legal right to change the will at any time. We Britishers have an absolute right to leave our property to whom we like – unlike some countries where the rights of children and other relatives to inherit a proportion of the estate are protected. Personally, after today, I feel the person who needs the protection is the one who makes the will.'

There was a degree of covert looking at each other, and stiffening in chairs. The meeting was finishing, but unsatisfactorily to most of the participants. Pat had got the message that the more she said, the less she advanced her cause. She was fighting on the side without weapons. She steamed out of the back door and started marshalling her children towards the car. Kit didn't tell her that he had seen the eldest of them listening at the kitchen door for most of the meeting. Dan was by now on the phone ordering a taxi, and when he put down the phone he turned to Wendy.

'I think I'll go outside and wait. I don't like the atmosphere in here.'

'Your going will improve it,' said Isla bitterly. 'Are you going to start looking for a job, now that you're back?'

'I'm talking to Bradford. Things look promising.'

'Bradford... Oh, the football club. Well, if that comes to nothing, be sure you register for unemployment benefit. It's not much, but you have expensive tastes and apparently no way of financing them. And I shouldn't think your lady friend brings anything into the household beyond two tits and an ever-open door. That looks like your taxi now.'

The room by then was well thinned out. Kit noticed the Honda driving off, leaving Micky still in the room. No doubt he was going to have the powwow with Kit that he had mentioned earlier. But the person who came up to him, obviously intent on making a point, was Ivor.

'Just in case you don't follow English football Kit, Bradford City Football Club is not in the top rank of English clubs, or even in the second rank. If Dan is not taken on by them he'll really be back in the Stanley Matthews era: ten pounds a week and your bus fare to the ground.'

Kit grinned.

'I rather thought I'd never heard of them. That sort of wage won't keep Wendy in lipsticks.'

'If he accepts a job like that, Wendy won't be around. I hear from Maria she was making advances to you at the family party. If that's true, lock up your wallet.'

'I will – and run a mile.'

'What I really wanted to say was that I'm sure Frank would never dare try to prove his non-parentage. If the medical evidence is sound – and Isla seemed quite sure – there's no other way he could get a court to accept his claim. Also, they'd want to know why he had waited twenty-odd years before he tried to shut you out in the cold.'

'That's what I thought. I suspect Frank's great pleasure in life is causing mayhem, and I doubt if he has any legal action in mind. On the other hand if he gets to hear about this morning's shenanigans he'll laugh his cruel laugh – at all of us, I suspect. My impression is that Frank feels superior to pretty well the whole human race.'

'So I've heard,' said Ivor. 'There's another point. Frank is – was? is? – a solicitor and he'd know better than most that going into law is a sure way of losing money ... and losing face as well.'

'He's not going to lose either if he can help it.'

'Well, I just thought I'd mention it... Wasn't Isla splendid, by the way?'

'Bang on target,' said Kit. 'And not at all the genteel upright type I've observed recently. This was another side of her altogether, and absolutely direct. You could say she stepped down into the gutter. But if you're dealing with filth you sometimes have to hurl some in reply.'

'You're thinking of Daniel, aren't you? Absolutely. He's been asking for it for years. Maybe she's been less illusioned about him than she pretended. Best of luck in what you're trying to do, Kit. I'll let Micky have his word.'

Micky had been lurking outside in the hall. He knew Kit had seen him there, so he had no compunction in saying: 'I can't say I thought Mum improved with plain speaking. I was waiting for four-letter words, though thank God they never came. It's not the mother I know at all.'

'I suppose it had to be strong for Dan to get the message. Whether she was really so soft about him in the past is maybe an open book. Ivor obviously thinks not, but you said he'd always been the favourite.'

'True. But I'm not the sharpest knife in the set. Anyway, I wanted to apologise for telling Pat what my father had told me... I mean, what he had alleged. When you've been married for a while you automatically tell your partner everything.'

Kit shook his head dubiously.

'I think that was true of my adoptive parents. I'd be willing to bet it was never true of Frank and Isla.'

'No, maybe not. Do you think that Isla ever knew that Frank doubted whether he was your father?'

Kit thought.

'I can't say she looked surprised. And she decided at once that he was the source of the rumour, and he'd told it to you so that you'd pass it on.'

'I'm the most likely one since I'm the only one to visit him... He was determined to tell

163

me, by the way. I'd hardly sat down before he said: "I had a visit from that imposter who's calling himself my son." Then he launched himself into it – it took up all the rest of the visit.'

'Did he make himself clear? Am I pretending to be Peter Novello, or was Peter Novello not his son?'

'The latter.'

'Why didn't he use that argument in the divorce?'

'There was no reason to. It was an amicable divorce, after some years of separation. Why would Dad proclaim himself a cuckold when there was no need to? And being a lawyer he was very susceptible to bad publicity, particularly publicity that came from a divorce case.'

'Fair enough. And especially as there was no child to examine and thus no medical evidence to back him up. He might have sounded like a man with a mania.'

'Frankly, that was what he sounded like to me,' said Micky, in a voice that had notes of tiredness and disgust.

'Oh?'

Micky looked down at his hands.

'I've always loved our mum, skated over the odd foible because we owe her so much. She brought us up single-handed, even before the separation. She gave us everything, and kept us on the rails. I don't want to think of her as having a bit on the side before the marriage broke down. I'd even have difficulty with it if it was afterwards, when she was a single mother, but I have real problems seeing it happen earlier, seeing her as a desperate housewife. She wouldn't have it off with anyone just to escape from the tedium of a stale marriage.'

'Is that how Frank described it?'

'He didn't describe it. He's a lawyer – he describes only what he saw and heard, things he knew thoroughly. That seemed to be the implication, though: taking a playboy to liven up a marriage gone wrong.'

'And who was the man – the one Frank obviously thinks fathered me?'

Micky grimaced.

'You're not going to believe this. It was an actor called Harry Bradley-Perle. He was in Leeds playing in *The Norman Conquests*. I vaguely remember the play because it's been on the television. The actor I don't remember ever seeing. I think I probably would remember if he'd been here at the house because this never was a place with people coming and going the whole time. Isla is naturally a private person and Frank is a lawyer and knows the dangers of indiscriminate talk to near strangers at parties. So I can't tell you much more about this.'

'You can't, for example, tell me where Harry and Isla supposedly first met,' asked

Kit, 'where they went to procreate, how long the alleged affair went on?'

'No, none of those. I wouldn't guarantee Frank knew either. You'd best ask Mum if you dare.'

'Oh, I'd dare. I've nothing to lose. But is that the best way to approach her? I wouldn't have thought so – at least, not until I have at least a bit of concrete information I can break to her, if there is any, and then go on from there.'

'That may be the best way, but do you have any choice?'

'What do you mean?'

'Everyone in there heard me say that we could talk later about Dad's accusations. If I know Mum, she'll have you over the grill before the day is out.'

And that was exactly what happened.

CHAPTER TEN

The Ones Who Got Away

'So what were you and Micky talking about this morning?' asked Isla, as they tucked into sirloin steak and the usual English off-season vegetables that same evening. Kit thought for a moment, chewed what he had already put in, then placed his knife and fork over the remains of his dinner.

'I think perhaps you could guess that,' he said, grinning.

'I certainly could not,' said Isla grimly. 'Why do you think I can guess the nonsense Frank has dreamt up when we've barely communicated in the last fifteen years?'

'Hmm,' said Kit, feeling rather lawyer-like. 'I don't know if it's nonsense or not, but I'm willing to bet it at least came up at the time of the marriage break-up.'

'Why should it? The divorce was "amicable" – which means we both wanted to get out of the marriage as quickly as possible and shot of each other. There was no reason why anything dirty should come up – not if it was something he'd thought up back then, and not if it was something that he's thought up in the years since, or some mad idea he's got about you, now he's lost his marbles.'

'I didn't suggest it came up in the legal matters surrounding the divorce, only in your personal relations with him. In fact, I bet it was something that had dominated those relations in the previous five or six years.'

'And that was?'

Kit prevaricated, then decided to bring it all out.

'The fact, if it is one, that Frank did not think he was my father: thought I was the product of a relationship that you had – if he's to be believed – with an actor with a poncy name which I can't recall now.'

There were several seconds of silence.

'Henry Bradley-Perle,' said Isla. 'Harry to his friends, of whom I was one and Frank emphatically was not. He was christened John Jones. So it's that old nonsense over again, is it? If you're sensible you won't give tuppence for that. Frank invented things to cover his own tastes and preferences. He thought we'd had enough children, so he clutched at the idea that I'd had an affair. Absolute nonsense. I was a good wife to him; all the priests said so at the time of the separation and divorce. They were trying to persuade me to keep the marriage going, of course. A little local fan club for Henry

Bradley-Perle was elevated into an affair. Well, take note: there was no affair. I was never unfaithful to Frank, which is a good deal more than he could say. You have been right all along: Frank Novello was – is – your father.'

Again there was silence while he thought this through, trying to make a guess at how much of it was true.

'So he invented the story to cover his own lack of enthusiasm for a third baby in the family. Is that what you mean?'

'Yes. Though the truth is he had very little love for any of his children, and had as little to do with any of them as he could. You've no doubt been told how he pretty well cast them off when we separated. There were a lot of bruised hearts over that.'

An idea occurred to Kit.

'Was a holiday in Italy a regular thing for the Novello family?'

Isla looked astonished.

'No. Why should it be? There was no regular place for our holidays. Most years we never got a holiday at all.'

'So the holiday in Trepalu was a one-off affair?'

'As near as makes no difference.'

'You didn't think it odd – an odd place, for example?'

'No. If I thought about it at all I'd have thought that Frank got a splendid bargain

169

from one of his clients.'

'Was he mean?'

'Only with his family. He could be quite lavish with spending on himself.'

Kit leant forward.

'I'm just trying out an idea on you. Frank Novello, stingy with his nearest and dearest, decides to take them on holiday. The place he chooses is in the remotest part of Italy, therefore among the most expensive to travel to. Sicily is also one of the most crime-riddled parts of the country, and was at that time riddled with petty crime and not so petty – blackmail, kidnapping, gang warfare, protection rackets. Why would any father choose, for a rare visit abroad, a part of the country which presented that sort of threat?'

Isla shrugged.

'I don't know. Perhaps he didn't know anything about the crime there.'

'Come off it, Isla. Everyone knows where the Mafia originated. Frank's name was Novello. His practice included criminal work. I've learnt that at some point in his career he played a biggish role in the gang warfare which plagues Glasgow – ostensibly his role was as a peacemaker and negotiator, but was it? Are you trying to tell me he was unaware of Sicily's criminal past and present?'

'It's not something that concerned me. I

never thought about it.'

'Well, I'm going to think about it. It seems to be possible that Frank arranged the holiday around the kidnapping of the third child in his family, a child he didn't much like or want. I'm not saying I'm sure about that, only saying there are an awful lot of question marks around that holiday, including: why did it take place at all, and why was it there? One other thing that I've only just thought of: at that date the police in Sicily were spectacularly corrupt. An advantage, especially when they insisted my abduction was a matter for their jurisdiction, and the English police went along with their claim, because technically it was true.'

'You may be right,' said Isla, collecting up plates. 'Heaven forfend I leap to the defence of my ex-husband. I've got fruit salad for dessert – does that suit you?'

Kit did not feel slapped down so much as circumvented. He kept the conversation on safe platitudes for the rest of the evening.

A day or two later Kit went along by appointment to the Millgarth police headquarters to have one of his regular chats with DS Hargreaves, who had got them a comfortable little interview room with coffee. Hargreaves sat himself on the table almost as a matter of course, as if placing his rugby-playing frame in a bullying proximity to the interlocutor was second nature to him.

'It's a good theory,' he said at the end of the discussion. 'So long as you acknowledge how far most of it is conjecture. And admit that conjecture is a complicated word for guesswork. There are two drawbacks that I can see.'

'What are they?'

'Almost impossible to prove at this distance of time.'

'I'm not planning on a criminal case,' said Kit. 'I just want to know the truth myself.'

'You will never know the truth if you content yourself with theory,' said Hargreaves. 'Theories are two a penny, evidence is worth its weight in gold.'

'There speaks a copper. But OK – point taken. And what's the other drawback?'

'Your theory takes us up to the point of your kidnapping. With Frank Novello taking his family to Sicily as part of a criminal plan. But it takes us no further. And what happened afterwards is in some ways the most puzzling thing of all.'

'Why do you say that?'

'How did you, as a result of the abduction, emerge as the adopted son – albeit probably not legally adopted – of a pair of sensitive, responsible, admirable people who were law-abiding to a fault and generally do-gooding. Do you get my point?'

'Yes. Don't mock them.'

'I'm not. I just sound as if I am when I use long words. Let's face it, you were fantastically lucky, and you've profited by what happened to you at the age of three to emerge happy, balanced, intelligent. To account for that we need to know something more about what happened after the abduction in Trepalu. What was the connection between your adoptive parents and whoever arranged the kidnapping?'

'What sort of thing do we need to know?'

'First and foremost, were you abducted to order, with your future with the Philipsons already mapped out?'

'Or?'

'Or were you abducted first, then made available for adoption, probably to people who were desperate to adopt but consistently turned down – age, past record, whatever the cause. Britain is very careful, where – say – the US hands kids over to film stars, drunks, druggy people with a whole chronicle of busted-up marriages and relationships. That, at any rate, is how the situation there looks from over here.'

'My mother used to say that most of the impressions British people have about the Americans are wrong.'

'Fair-minded as well as all the rest,' said Hargreaves with a lopsided grin. 'Oh well, mebbe, as the Scots say.' He heaved himself off the table and started collecting notebooks and files.

'Here, you're not going yet, are you?' asked Kit.

'Yes. You forget, kiddie, that I'm a policeman, and not a private eye. I'm paid by the municipality, not by a casual private client who wants his past, his wife or his dog's past looked into.'

'Isn't there any other possible connection between the Novello family and Jürgen and Genevieve?'

Hargreaves stopped by the door.

'Any number, I would guess. Possibilities I haven't thought about because I'm not a thinker by nature. One thing occurs to me – as sort of halfway house between the two I've just mentioned. Is it possible that you were taken so that you could be offered to the Philipsons in order to entrap them into a situation where they could be forced to do something, or forced to wink at something other people have done – for fear of losing you, the precious child they had longed for all their married life?'

Kit thought.

'I suppose so. Though I never got the feeling of their being entrapped.'

'Think it through. And get to know more about the Philipsons: the English people who adopted them in 1939, their families in Germany or Austria who sent them on the Kindertransport to save their lives, find out about their careers and occupations when they grew up.'

He seemed to be forgetting, Kit thought, that only Jürgen was German by birth.

Two days later Kit was just beginning to recover from one of Isla's English, or rather British breakfasts. It was an example of excess that he was considering giving up, especially as Isla refused to excuse him from more than two of the eight items on her choice list.

'I'll have a boiled egg tomorrow,' he said, patting his new belly.

'Two,' said Isla. 'With some good, buttery soldiers.'

'No, I want–'

But at that point the telephone rang.

'Kit,' came the well-known voice of Hargreaves, 'I've been thinking–'

'You said you never did.'

'I didn't quite say that. I've been muddling about with my brain on the subject of your adoptive father.'

'Jürgen. Yes.'

'He was adopted by an English family after coming here in the Kindertransport – Kids' transport. And that adoption was very successful – right?'

'Right. My grandparents – or adoptive grandparents, as I now know – were really nice people.'

'I've been thinking that the success of his own adoption meant that Jürgen was pre-disposed towards adoption, and willing to consider some way of bringing it about for him and his wife – some way that was a bit dicey.'

Kit considered.

'I suppose that's a possibility. Where does it take us?'

'You've never told me if he made this Kindertransport journey on his own, or whether he had brothers or sisters with him.'

'A sister. She was eight at the time, so he was certainly dependent on her.'

'I'm sure she would have contributed to the success of the Philipsons' adoption.'

'Oh, no question of it. Jürgen always paid tribute to her.'

'I'm guessing she's no longer alive.'

'No, she died a few months after Jürgen. She had heart problems most of her life. Hilda was her name – with an "e" in the German form. If she was still alive I could cut a number of corners, because I think she must have known almost everything about Jürgen's life and opinions. She was nice too. I liked her. We saw her every year, in the summer, and she always brought me a well-considered present. The way to a child's heart...'

'No living husband?'

'No husband at all.'

'Partner, lover, flatmate?'

'She lived with another cashier at the bank. Female. With or next to, in neighbouring flats, I think. Sorry, I should have mentioned what she did for a living. She and this flatmate both worked for Coutts' bank – very old, rather posh, and definitely exclusive. The head branch is in the Strand.'

'I know them. We have a branch in Leeds.'

'Anyway she and this friend – Binkie her name was – both lived in this large house in Twickenham.'

'Of the lesbian persuasion, I'm guessing.'

'I have no idea. Genuinely – I'm not trying to hide anything. I saw her friend once or twice when she came up with Aunt Hilda to the Edinburgh Festival. But I wouldn't have understood what lesbianism was, and I wouldn't have been able to interpret the signs, so you can forget all the usual jokes.'

'Don't be so bloody self-righteous. Actually I've always been a great supporter of women's rugby. It gives us something to talk about. I sometimes have problems with that, with women.'

'I can imagine.'

'Sarkiness will get you nowhere. Anyway, if they lived together, Hilda's early life, her family, must surely have come up for discussion.'

'I'd imagine so. But how can I get in touch? I can't even remember the friend's surname – or her real Christian name, come to that.'

'Ring Coutts' bank. Talk to the personnel department.'

The more Kit thought about the idea the more he liked it. The person he spoke to in the personnel department was one of those people that old-fashioned firms run to – the one who'd been there since she left school.

'Hilda Philipson,' she said. 'Oh yes, I knew her well. Lovely person: always smiling, though she'd had more than her share of ill health, and always ready to help. I can tell you she was a great loss – to atmosphere as much as anything else.'

'Yes, that's how I remember her. I'm her nephew. My own parents have died in the last few years, and there's something come up that I think Hilda may have talked over with Binkie.'

'Oh, dear old Binkie!'

'I'm afraid I don't remember her real name.'

'Barbara Southcott. Are you wanting to contact her?'

'Yes, I am.'

'Just send a letter to us here, with PLEASE FORWARD on it. I'll keep an eye on the post and make doubly sure that it gets to her.'

'I'll write today.'

Two days later he received a phone call

from Binkie – brusque but definitely friendly. Two days after that he was sitting in her front room in Twickenham, and she was ministering from a tray of tea and cakes.

'I know from what you told me on the phone,' said the rather old-fashioned-looking woman, probably in her late sixties, 'that you are looking into the circumstances of your adoption by Jürgen and Genevieve and you'd welcome any light Hilda may have thrown on the matter in conversation with me. Forgive me if I say that I'm used to and comfortable with the idea of an adopted child wishing to find out and make contact with his birth parents. The adopted child who wishes to find out about his adoptive parents seems a much odder phenomenon.'

She spoke precisely, almost pedantically. An ideal witness, Kit thought.

'I understand your bewilderment,' he said, matching his tone to hers. 'Can we just say for the moment that, to the best of my knowledge, I was abducted from my birth parents at the age of three, while they were on holiday in Sicily.'

He said no more. Binkie's face showed her shock. Then she shook herself and put her hand on his to show she trusted his account.

'Ask what you like,' she said.

'Right. And thank you. How much did you know about Hilda's German background?'

'Not much. Nothing ordered. What I

mean is we never sat down and talked about what happened chronologically. It was just a question of things coming up – when talking with me, with people at work, even with the local clergyman. I'm a churchgoer, by the way, but Hilda was a non-believer. Never practised Judaism.'

'Perhaps not surprisingly,' said Kit. 'What kind of things came out in these conversations?'

'Little things. Like having a ticket collector on the train to London with a kindly smile. "Somehow I knew from him that it was going to be all right," she said. "We'd had so few kindly smiles at home."'

'Did she say much about her mother and father?'

'The memories of them were mostly of her mother. Naturally. The memories I best remember her mentioning were of the days and weeks after Kristallnacht. Somebody rang her mother, and when she put the phone down – because you had to be very careful what you said on the phone – she turned to Hilda and Jürgen and clasped her hands: "They offered the people coffee and sandwiches. Think of it! They were welcoming!"'

'Who was she talking about? Who were "the people"?'

'The people who were applying for permits to go to Britain. And other places too –

America, Australia and so on. After "the night of glass" the queue stretched along the streets around British embassies and consulates in all the bigger towns like Frankfurt. And when the applicants got into the consulates they were treated kindly – fed, given good advice, which was even more welcome. If you got a residence permit for the whole family you might get, for example, a husband or wife out of custody if they'd been arrested, or even if they'd been sent to a camp. At that stage the Nazis wanted to be rid of the Jews by emigration more than they wanted to kill them.'

Kit was silent for a moment.

'So far Hilda's memories seem almost happy ones.'

Binkie considered this.

'They mostly were. They were the only ones Hilda could cherish, the ones that enabled her, privately, to look into the darker ones. I remember her saying: "You can't believe the fear we felt." That was the only time that she mentioned the terrible things she had seen.'

'Did her mother try to leave Germany with the children?'

'Yes, she did, but she was not successful. She was the daughter of a very influential – once influential – rabbi. Maybe that was the reason – a family literate, educated, used to political action. Dangerous to let out abroad.

Anyway, for the rest of 1938 and the first half of 1939 she put all her strength into getting the children to England, and strengthening Hilda's nerve and resolve and trying to see potential danger and difficulties.'

'What about the father?'

'Ah yes – the father...' She took a sip of her tea. 'Hilda almost never mentioned her father except once, when she said he helped to get permits for her and Jürgen.'

'Why not mention him, then?'

'Of course it could be mainly because he was almost never there – seldom at least. That was in Frankfurt, where the family had always lived. He, I think, was in Vienna.'

'You would have thought that, if the mother couldn't get out herself, the obvious person to go with the children was the father. If he'd been arrested she might have joined the queues to get an exit visa for him.'

'Yes. You might have thought that. I think there must have been some reason, though. Why she didn't do that, I mean.'

'What makes you say that?'

'Because Hilda once said, not long before she died, and said it as if it was a tribute to her mother, not a criticism: "At least she didn't try to get a permit for father. She never joined a queue for him."'

Kit looked at Binkie, and Binkie looked back at him. Both were wondering what was the significance of the gnomic praise.

CHAPTER ELEVEN

Transport

'Think of it,' said Binkie, pouring out another cup of tea and handing Kit a plate of cake. 'Think of the bravery of the woman – sending her children out to completely unknown futures. And don't just think of the bravery – think of the desolation.'

'Yes, I was imagining the figure of the mother,' admitted Kit, nodding vigorously. 'Was she allowed to see the children off? Was she on the platform pretending the separation would only be for a short time? Inevitably one fixes on her, rather than on the father who was ... well, what was he doing? Flitting around Germany or Europe as a whole? In hiding somewhere?'

Binkie did not answer at once.

'And what about the children too?' she said at last. 'Particularly Hilda. She was just old enough to understand, but not really to understand in depth. Think of the desolation she must have felt! And the sense of being deserted by both parents – understanding that at least her mother knew it was for the best, the only possible escape, in fact, but still feeling that she was being shunted off.'

'Did she show signs of bitterness towards her mother, then?'

'Never,' said Binkie forcefully, obviously regretting bringing that matter up. 'Ignore what I said. Treat it as a piece of amateur psychoanalysis: that that was what she must have felt, though I have no evidence at all that she did.'

'But of course, you knew her much later, when she must have come to see things more deeply, more clearly.'

'That's true.'

'Was she the complete English girl when you first came to know her?' asked Kit.

'On the surface,' said Binkie cautiously. 'She'd been in England twelve years by then. No accent, nothing one could clutch on to that was foreign. Oh no ... there was one thing I did notice, one odd thing: the fact that if anyone surprised her, by, for example, coming up behind her and speaking to her, she would not only jump (we might all do that), but her face would be taken over entirely by fear, by blank terror.'

There was a silence for a few seconds in the room. Then Kit said: 'I see. How horrible. Did that make you think?'

'In a limited sort of way. I assumed she might have been bombed in the Blitz. But I never asked her, not then. And even as things came out I never asked. In our circles that was something one did not do. I just hoped things would emerge.'

'And I'm guessing that they did. Was there any occasion that you remember particularly?'

Binkie put her cup down and leant against the back of her chair, breathing hard.

'I remember the Coronation,' she said at last. '1953. We were all wild with patriotic fervour: it was the beginning of a new age, we thought. Though with Mr Churchill as prime minister and Mr Attlee as leader of the opposition it was really the old men having their last throw. We couldn't, of course, afford any of the places on offer on the route: rooms like that were fetching what then seemed like a fortune. We had to find a position on the Mall near Buckingham Palace the moment we left work the day before and hold it all night. That meant we saw the procession, kept the position for the period of the service in the abbey (some people had portable radios we could listen to it on), then we saw the procession back to the palace, the queen wearing her crown now, and then the appearances on the balcony and all that. Thrilling!'

'It must have been an exciting day.'

'Oh it was – marvellous. But one thing I remember was when we were making plans. We were going through everything we must do, rather envying those who had an easier berth, and I said: "It's worth it, putting up with a bit of hardship." And out came from Hilda: "You don't know what hardship is. You haven't been a Jew in Nazi Germany." I was flabbergasted. I just stammered: "I'm so sorry, I didn't know," and she said: "Forget I said it." But of course, I never did. Couldn't. But it made me wonder, all the time, what she had been through, and how she had escaped from it.'

'And what did she tell you?'

'Just disconnected bits. The remark about feeling fear "all the time". A remark about her religion, which was almost an accusation that I could hold on to mine whereas someone who'd gone through the persecution and murder of the Jews could not.'

'What did she say?'

'Oh, it was probably in one of the long intervals on Coronation Day as we stood along the parade route with nothing very much happening – yes, I'm sure that's when it was. I mentioned what the radio said was going on behind the scenes, and I commented priggishly that it was a central part of the religious meaning of the Coronation. And she said: "Oh, I've given up all that." I asked what she meant by "all that" and she said: "Religion and all that. You can't have a faith, and certainly not a belief in the Jews as the chosen race, if you've lived through

186

the Holocaust and lost all the people you loved." And I said: "I suppose not," and thought how feeble and inadequate it sounded.'

'Did the conversation go any further?'

'I felt it had to, so in another of the intervals I asked her when her mother died and how she knew. She said: "The occupying powers were very good at getting out information. She is believed to have died in Dachau." "And did your father – did you lose him too?" I asked, never sure how these things were best put. She replied: "I don't know. As good as.'"

'And was that all she ever said about her father?'

Binkie was silent for a time.

'I don't know... There was a time, much later... This was a time, you understand, when we were much closer. Not sexually, because we neither of us wanted that. We were friends in the fullest and loveliest sense, and that was enough. This must have been ...oh ... early Seventies. We were in Vienna for the opera, and she'd told me earlier that her father had been there for a time, but had slipped away after the outbreak of war, to Italy. How she knew that, I don't know. But in one of the intervals of the opera – it was *Fidelio* – she said, almost apropos of nothing: "One has to beware of charm. It's the most dangerous thing. And it's not just handsome, amusing people who have it. There are hideous, misshapen, outrageously twisted people, and they have charm, and – bang! – they bring disaster." I just murmured: "You're right," and left it at that.'

'But you connected the comment with her father? Was this because he'd been in Austria before the German takeover?'

'Not just that. But I'd never had the idea that Hilda had memories of her father. Now it seemed as though she had. Or – this is just a way-out guess – had met him during that holiday we took in Austria in 1971.'

'By appointment, so to speak?'

'Yes, maybe.'

'What would give you that impression?'

Binkie thought hard, trying to be careful, precise in her thought.

'Usually when we went away on holiday we did most things together. It just happened like that, naturally. I had my interest in religion, Hilda had her interest in Nazism and the war, and her family background. But this time we did less together. Hilda would say she had something "on", and I accepted that without question.'

'She could have been conducting research,' said Kit.

'Yes, I thought of that – but why not tell me, discuss it with me, bring me in on it? And I don't think she'd have found it easy.

The Austrians were very cagey at that time about their past. Their complicity with the Nazis was a well-kept secret, at least until recently.'

'You didn't see her together with a man of the right age to be her father, then?' asked Kit.

'No... Or I don't think so... I did one day see someone ahead of me with someone who could have been Hilda, and I sped up. We were all on the Schulerstrasse. And then I suddenly thought: "What am I doing. ?What business is it of mine if she doesn't want to make it my business?" And I felt cheap.'

'You just saw the back of this man?'

'Yes, that's all.'

'How old would her father have been then?'

'Hilda was born in 1931 and he could have been say twenty then – or fifty, come to that. If it was twenty he would have been around sixty when I saw them – if it was them. And he'd be ninety or a hundred now.'

There was silence as Kit thought. It was Binkie who broke it.

'We're into the realm of wild conjecture now. Are we allowed to stay in it?'

'Of course.'

'It's just that if we don't discuss it now, we might never. It's one thing chatting over tea and cakes, quite another to put your impressions, and your conjectures from them, down on paper.'

'Of course, you're right. 'What does your conjecture spring from?'

'Nothing. An impression. It concerns the Greenspan marriage.'

'I see,' said Kit. 'Not much of a marriage by all accounts. At least, by the late Thirties they hardly ever saw each other – is that right?'

'Yes. But that may have been the fate of a lot of marriages at that time. If one half of the marriage – usually the husband – was a likely target for arrest, interrogation, torture, execution, then he might well keep away from his family.'

'Is that the impression you got from Hilda?'

'No, it's not. From the little Hilda said, my impression is that her mother didn't talk about the marriage and her husband unless she was forced to. When she did talk it was probably very guarded, maybe even ambiguous. She certainly didn't try to arouse in the little girl admiration or devotion for the absent parent. I think Hilda may have felt her mother was unjust: that there was suspicion and even hatred between the pair, and it was not all Walter Greenspan's fault.'

'Right. Anything more?'

'I toyed with the idea that there might not have been a marriage at all. At most a liaison, maybe just a love affair, brief, and leaving an undercurrent of recrimination.'

'Remember there were two offspring, five years apart.'

'True. A liaison, then, on and off, but enduring.'

'Can't you dredge your memory and come up with some of the things that made you guess there was no marriage?'

'I suppose I could try... The fact that Frau Greenspan made no attempt to get her husband out of the country. And I had the impression that she made hardly any attempt to leave with the children herself. I thought it was probably made clear to her early on that there was no question of her getting special treatment if she was not a married woman.'

'That sounds possible,' said Kit. 'The sort of proviso that politicians made at that time to secure Church approval.'

'And think of the dilemma that would face the poor mother: the only way she could save her children would be to get rid of them – separate them entirely from herself. And the children would probably not understand, particularly if their illegitimacy was kept generally secret.'

'Which it surely would have been, in that time and place,' said Kit. He sighed. 'If only Hilda was still alive.'

'Yes. I think that every day of my life. For

purely selfish reasons, I'm afraid. But if she had lived she would have been able to tell us everything – or at least everything a child might understand.'

'It may be that a child in those times, that place, didn't have very long to enjoy un-clouded childhood,' said Kit.

'I suppose a specimen of her writing wouldn't help,' said Binkie without much hope in her voice.

'It might,' said Kit, though he couldn't think of any ways it could. 'Do you have letters, then?'

'Not letters, no. We were almost always together, you see. And if we hadn't been I don't suppose I'd have kept her letters, or she mine. Two boring bank cashiers... No, it's a diary.' She saw Kit's face lighting up with anticipation, but she immediately damped it down. 'Not for the years in Frankfurt. I hoped for that and would have read it if it had been.'

'How did you come to have it?'

'I was executor of Hilda's will. I'd done everything else – the money to an Anglo-Jewish Society; the furniture and books to Shelter and so on. The remainder to me. She knew you would have enough from your parents. We'd discussed it in advance, and I'd practically written the will. When I found the diary I took it and wondered what to do with it. Jürgen was dead by that time and I knew Genevieve was ill – she'd written me such a nice, brave letter. I suppose eventually I would have offered it to you, but the truth is I forgot it. It's all about life with the Philipsons, you see. Not very interesting, and not at all useful.'

She got up. Kit admired the precision and elegance of her steps as she went out of the room – what an asset she must have been to the atmosphere at Coutts'! Soon she came back with a cheaply bound exercise book: the cover was almost khaki, and the pages were that grubby brown that spoke of wartime and restrictions, at least until recently, when that same brownness of cheap paper began to affect books again. She put it into his hand.

'There. Take it. It's yours. If you have any questions ring me or come again. I may know more about the Philipsons than you do, unless Jürgen talked about them a lot to you.'

'He didn't. Very seldom, but always admiring and grateful. He'd have been taught to be that by Hilda as a child. I met the Philipsons a few times when they were very old and I was very young. What impressions there are remaining are of very kind, amiable people.'

He got up to go.

'Good luck,' said Binkie.

'I need it,' said Kit. But being a young

man he added: 'But sometimes that's when it comes along.'

Kit sat in his small, utilitarian hotel bedroom – he had no desire to minister to the monstrous greed of most London hoteliers – and looked at the diary he had been given. He had glanced at the first page on the Underground. It had started in the middle of a sentence: '*...before we had been made to sit on our own. After that none of the children talked to me. It is so different here. Full of shortages and what we call "make-do-and-mend" but all the children talk, and are happy usually, and ask about Germany, and Jews, and my family. I can't tell them much. I try to forget.*'

His heart had sunk immediately. He didn't see himself getting much information from a child who was living in England and trying to forget. In any case her early years must have schooled her in not writing about the things most interesting to her, for fear of their coming into the hands of Hitler's hirelings.

And as he read the first pages his hunch that nothing would be found about Hilda and Jürgen's earlier years in Germany was confirmed. It was all about school: Miss Lucas's kindness, Miss Campbell-Jeffries' strictness, the fact that she was second in class in English (this was marked with an exclamation mark). Kit paid tribute to her diligence and flair: the school was in Hampstead – the competition would have been fierce.

Periodically there was an odd remark about the Philipsons: *'Auntie May understanding as ever'; 'Uncle Theo and Jürgen played cricket, and the latter picked it up very quickly'; 'A wonderful birthday cake – where does Auntie get the stuff? I asked her. She smiled and didn't say.'* All the remarks were affectionate and spoke of the Philipsons' skill in earning the children's trust and love.

It was ten pages into the diary when there came a note on the entry for January 1st: *'New Year 1943. War going better.'* Kit had decided two pages earlier that that was where Binkie had given up the diary. The dust on the later pages was more pervasive than that on the earlier first five or six pages (three or four entries per page). So Hilda by then would have been about twelve or thirteen. A very accomplished and thinking twelve or thirteen, but that was natural in the circumstances. So was the feeling of greater freedom in the writing. Freedom was working its liberating spell.

'May no longer feels she has to walk me to school,' ran an entry on March 4th. *'I'm pleased – she has enough calls on her time, and she is not young. Not like Mutti – though Mutti never seemed young. The cares she bore had worn her down. Every time May has stood in*

195

the doorway now to see me off, I have been reminded of my last sight of Mutti. We had had to say goodbye in a mucky old field near to the Frankfurt railway station. Parents were not allowed on the platform. I suppose the officials were afraid that so many grieving parents seeing their children off to a foreign country that welcomed them might rouse a general sympathy for the parents and children in their plight. I don't think! I never remember arousing the least sympathy in people who knew us but were not Jews – however tragic the things that happened to me were.

'So I remembered stopping with Jürgen at the door into the station and, turning round, being just close enough to see the tears streaming down our mother's face. She tried to wipe them quickly away.

'I contrast this with May and her happy wave and proud smile. This is what living in a democracy means: safety. She still takes Jürgen to school, of course: he is only seven, but his primary school is only two streets away and he could easily go on his own if he needed to. But May is too conscientious to fail him, as my dear mother would never have failed us.

'If only she had not told me...'

There was nothing more than that, nothing to explain the remark. No doubt the young Hilda knew she would not need reminders of what it was.

The diary entries ran from November

1942 to March 1944. Entries became scrappier as time went by, and Kit suspected that Hilda was feeling more and more at home in her new country, had fewer and fewer memories (almost none of them good ones) of her former homeland. The only good memory was her mother – comparisons of her and May, a few words each, memories of her tenderness towards Jürgen, who was a shy child. One that was a little longer came in April 1943.

'*24th. Today it is three years since we heard from our mother. I said nothing to Jürgen. He has almost no memories of her. There was a letter, of course. But I could not ... the truth is I could not think of it as a letter from her. Reading it in 1940 I could not hear her voice or feel the tenderness of her embrace. It was so completely lacking in any reminder of her that I decided it must have been a simple copy of a standard letter that all Jewish parents had to write out. I say "all Jewish parents" and I mean "in the camp" because I am convinced Mutti has been arrested or interned. I described the letter to Magda Cohen, the only other Kindertransport child at Heathside School. She said she had had one similar, but had thrown it away. She thought to keep it would be a sort of victory for Hitler and his gang. I saw her point, but I could never have thrown mine away. It did have one reminder of her: her lovely round handwriting.*'

There was another entry that caught Kit's

eye on that first reading of Hilda's diary. The date was July 11th 1943, and Hilda went into capitals to announce the news:

ENGLISH AND US TROOPS INVADE ITALY.

'Yes! It's true. They have landed in Sicily and are going to push their way up the country, ridding it for all time of Germans. I am so happy! I would pray to my God if I knew which one He is, and if I knew whether I believed at all. I hope that big creep Mussolini is quaking in his boots.'

At this point Hilda left a few lines of space, perhaps to fill in any later news if any should be made public. Nothing apparently was. On the line under the space Hilda had written: *'I wish my mother had never told me those things about our father.'*

CHAPTER TWELVE

Only Connect

'Binkie?'

'Yes. Hello Kit.'

'You have a good ear for voices. I wouldn't be so complimentary about your reading of manuscripts.'

'Oh Lord – did I miss something? I'm so sorry, Kit–'

'Don't be. It gave me the joy of discovering something for myself. You didn't exactly miss anything. It's just that you gave up too early.'

'Did I? It was some time in 1942 or early the next year. I thought she was never going to go back to pre-war days.'

'She does, though – mostly in isolated sentences. I think she was emotionally liberated to dig up memories by the preparations for the Allied invasion of Europe, starting in southern Italy. It actually happened in July 1943. Probably if you expected a German invasion of your sanctuary you would suppress memories of that country, or at least be careful about writing them down. But then came the hope that the war would soon be over – though it wasn't – and that Germany would be defeated, as it was. And with that hope came a slight loosening of all the inhibitions about writing down things from her Frankfurt past. Just phrases, you understand, odd sentences.'

'For example?' came Binkie's voice, eagerly.

'"I wish my mother had never told me those things about our father."'

There was silence, and then: 'Good Lord.'

'Yes. Does that chime in with anything she ever said to you?'

'Not at all. I told you, or I implied: she said very little. It's a difficult sentence to interpret, isn't it? Is she talking about her father as a family man? As a husband and father? Or is she talking about him as a social or political animal – a Jew, an opponent of the regime, a plotter?'

'Don't know,' said Kit, thinking that Binkie could make a more informed guess than he could. 'The context doesn't give any clues – there's a blank left after the invasion of Sicily, then that. Is there anyone she would be most likely to talk to about her father? A Jew perhaps – a Jewish girl, or even a boyfriend?'

'No...' said Binkie. 'Or rather, what I really mean is, I don't know. For example, I thought last night, not being able to get off to sleep, about another friend of Hilda's –

one whom I never met, though Hilda talked about her now and then. She called her Nora, but I think her name must have been Leonora – or perhaps Leonore with an "e", as Hilda was really Hilde with an "e".'

'She was German?'

'Austrian. She worked in the embassy in a slightly odd capacity because she wasn't your usual embassy staff member, part of the diplomatic service. She was Austrian by birth, a British resident long ago naturalised, and she acted as some kind of liaison or advisor to Austrian residents in Britain.'

'I see,' said Kit slowly. 'Or rather, I don't quite. Why should they need a special advisor? And Hilda wasn't an Austrian citizen, ever.'

'No. But there was some kind of slant on her job. It was mainly to do with finding and honouring Austrians who had opposed the takeover of the country by the Nazis in 1938, the *Anschluss* – opposed it by leaving, sometimes by working from within, or by simply being Jews and dying in the concentration camps in the years before 1945. The job was suddenly made for her at the time when Europe needed to feel better about their role in the Second World War.'

'This sounds interesting. Especially as Hilda may have seen her father in Austria or he may have had some Austrian connection.'

'Exactly,' said Binkie cheerfully. 'In any

case the only point I'm making is that this friend may have been the one who brought the father and daughter together.'

'Do you know her age? Is she likely to be still alive?'

'My impression is that she was a year or two older than Hilda. No reason why she shouldn't be alive.'

'And no reason why she shouldn't be dead,' said Kit cheerfully. 'But it's worth a try. I'll get on to the embassy.'

'Good luck with that. And could you give me another look at the diaries?'

'I'm itching to. I'm interested in anything that helps me to know Hilda better.'

Kit's instinct, in matters that concerned his adoptive family, was to act at once. When he put down the phone he got on to Directory Enquiries and was told the number of the Austrian embassy. He introduced himself as the son of a man who had been on one of the Kindertransport trains. The voice at the other end was slightly bored, as if she had heard from all too many such.

'I think the person you want to speak to is Mrs Madison.'

'I was given the name of Leonore or Nora.'

'That's right. English people usually settle for Nora. She's in today, and she has some spare time. Would you like me to fit you into the three o'clock slot? That would give you up to an hour of her time.'

'Please do slot me in. My name is Christopher Philipson. I'll be there at ten to three.'

He examined his mental list of things he might take in during his London visit, and decided to go to the exhibition of Flemish art at the Queen's Gallery. He thought it might prove soothing but he was, in fact, intensely excited by so many rarely seen masterpieces, and his mind was all the time on his mother, Genevieve, and how she would have illuminated the pictures for him. It was with a sense of impending revelations that he walked from the Underground station to the embassy, and this stomach-churning excitement grew in his ten-minute wait outside the door of 'Leonore Madison, Special Advisor on Citizenship'.

The office he was ushered into was like a well-used domestic sitting room, complete with TV, bookcases and easy chairs. There was a desk, but it was humanised by the substantial woman who sat behind it. She must, Kit felt, be at least seventy, but the eyes in her turtle-like face were alive with interest and enjoyment of life. The face was sallow, minimally but carefully made-up, and Kit was pretty sure she was wearing a wig.

'Thank you for seeing me. My name is–'

'Philipson. Yes, I have your name in front of me. It interests me because it is not common.'

'No, it's not. And I believe you have been

a friend of my aunt.'

She smiled a smile of self-satisfaction.

'Ah, so I am right. Dear Hilda. Yes, we were friends. Not close, intimate friends, you understand: people who shared every mood, every secret. No, we weren't that, but we did enjoy each other's company. She first came to me years ago with a problem, or let's call it an enquiry, and we stayed friends for the rest of her life.'

'Am I allowed to know what the enquiry was about?'

She raised her hand, palm outwards. She was no pushover.

'Hold your horses, young man! Maybe, and maybe not. First I want to know who I'm talking to.'

Kit nodded.

'I'm the son of Jürgen Philipson, Hilda's brother, who was, like her, one of the Kindertransport children.'

'And, of course, the adopted son of the Philipsons, having originally in Germany been called Greenspan. Jürgen no doubt found adoption of you easy to contemplate – which is not always the case among those from Central and Eastern Europe – because he had been successfully adopted himself. Because you were adopted by him and his wife, weren't you?'

'Yes, I was. I wasn't trying to hide that. The fact is, it's rather complicated, with lots of blank spaces.'

'Finding one's birth mother is very common these days, especially if the adoption went through the usual channels.'

Kit was disconcerted but heartened by her acumen.

'I've already found my birth mother, even though the adoption didn't go through the "usual channels", as you call them. I'm perhaps misleading you when I call it an adoption at all.'

'So what happened to put you into Jürgen Philipson's care – excellent care, so Hilda always said?'

'Yes, excellent care, from both him and his wife, my mother. The complicating factor is that I became "available" as a result of abduction.'

She looked at him as if the world had turned upside down, then she whistled.

'You mean you were kidnapped? At Jürgen's instigation?'

'Kidnapped, yes. At his instigation? I would very much doubt that. Jürgen was the most upstanding, the most moral person I've ever known.'

A glint came into Nora Madison's eye.

'Have you thought of selling your story to the Walt Disney Corporation? He likes British pantomime plot lines.'

Kit, after a moment's pause, laughed heartily.

'*Cinderella, Jack and the Beanstalk, Dick Whittington?* I've seen those. And does *Peter Pan* count? Yes, there is a sort of make-believe aspect to my story, in its early stages. I remember little from the abduction.'

'How old were you?'

'I was only three, the same age my father was when he took the train to England with Hilda. I remember my nursery, the pictures on the walls, and the smell of my birth mother when she'd been cooking.'

'Not bad for a start. So what about your birth mother? You say you've found her. Is she happy to have you back?'

'Deliriously.'

'And happy you are making enquiries into the abduction?'

Kit shrugged, hiding his unease. 'I suspect she thinks it's a waste of time. I'm back, she's got me home, and I've got her. We have time to get to know each other. I imagine she thinks I ought to be satisfied with that.'

'I'd have thought ... well, never mind. I don't know her, do I? What do you know about the abduction?'

'That's the point – almost nothing. The people who did it I never saw again. Correction: I never remember seeing them again. Almost all my early memories are of Genevieve and Jürgen and a succession of au pairs. But odd things seem to attach themselves to the abduction. There was a confrontation between Jürgen and my birth father at a conference in Glasgow a few years ago.'

'Who and what is – or was – your birth father?'

'Frank Novello, a solicitor in Leeds. He has got some sort of reputation through sorting out rivalries between the various gangs – mostly of Italian origin – in Glasgow. He, my birth father, is a sardonic, mischief-making kind of man – to me not the peacemaking sort at all. When I went to see him recently he seemed to deny that he is my father, and he's said similar things to others. That is all rather odd, because he made no such assertions at the time of my birth parents' separation or the divorce, which happened two or three years after the abduction.'

Nora looked intrigued, as if this were the sort of problem that she enjoyed.

'Interesting. So how does Hilda come into this?'

'She doesn't. But that rather dramatic confrontation I mentioned, at the conference in Glasgow – from what I know about Jürgen there are two things that occur to me as possible grounds for the disagreement.'

'And these are?'

'First me. Jürgen, either knowingly or un-knowingly, accepted a child who had been abducted and made that child his own. Perhaps Novello was threatening to take me away.'

'Interesting still, though lots of un-answered questions occur to me. Go on.'

'Here's how you can perhaps help me. I have very little information about Jürgen and Hilda's birth father. Hilda's journal – we have just two years of it, while she was living with the Philipsons but before they legally adopted her – reveals that Hilda's mother, before Hilda left on the train, had told her something upsetting about her father: the mother's husband, or perhaps her lover, her seducer or whatever.'

'Something to his discredit?'

'That seems very likely. Hilda says she wishes she had not been told whatever it was.'

'There is something rather ugly about one parent setting children against the other parent.'

'Yes. And we do not learn from the diary or from anywhere else that Hilda's mother was unpleasant by nature – quite the reverse. And when you think about it, and the circumstances in which the revelation to the daughter was made, it possibly was done only reluctantly, as a necessity.'

'I see what you mean. That if the mother found herself trapped in Germany, with the concentration camps the only prospect–'

'The camps which Jews were beginning to

hear about, even though other Germans managed apparently to remain ignorant of them till 1945. The mother might have feared that the children would find themselves in England and being reclaimed by their father. If she had good reason to think that such a reunion would be a disaster, then she might have felt she had to issue a warning – impressing it on the child at a crucial moment in her life, when she was departing for a new country.'

'And the child might understand her gesture in a quite different way.'

'How do you mean?'

'She thinks she is being set against her father, at this crucial, highly emotional moment, and she feels this is wrong – mean.'

'That sounds convincing. But she was only eight...'

'Agreed, but she hadn't had the experience of a normal eight-year-old. She must have been terribly lacking in things – people – to cling to.'

'And she clung to her father, the idea of her father, because otherwise she had only her mother, whom she was losing that very day.'

Nora mulled over that for a while.

'Yes. That seems to me a possibility,' she said at last.

'I take your point about people to cling to, because I think Jürgen tried to be completely self-reliant for the same reason. You, who knew Hilda quite well, must have sensed the same reaction in her.'

'I knew Hilda superficially well.'

'Did you talk often about her father?'

'I wouldn't say often, but we did talk.'

'Did you get the impression of her resenting her mother's trying to manipulate her attitude to her father?'

Nora Madison hesitated.

'I suppose I must have. But the idea only came to me now, as a result of hearing about the diaries. I have no doubt that Hilda loved her mother very much, but I think she also wanted to think well of her father.'

'Maybe that's true of most children. Emotionally she was cut in half, as I see it.'

'I wouldn't want to exaggerate this feeling towards her father, whom she virtually never knew. If she had met him – which she may well have done – and if he had made an unpleasant or irresponsible impression on her – his behaviour generally does suggest a strain of irresponsibility – she would have discarded him without any hesitation as he in her babyhood had discarded her. But she would have gone to the meeting hoping not to have to do that.'

'Yes, that does make sense. But did she tell you about a meeting?'

'Oh no. And I never would have asked her. I helped her with family things but I didn't participate.'

'But did you find out anything about her father? That is how you came together, isn't it?'

'Yes, that's right. Hilda remembered her mother saying her father was in Vienna, remembered her waiting for letters with Austrian stamps. That's why Hilda first came to see me.'

'So you took this ... this case, this enquiry on board and tried to find out about her father and his fate.'

'That roughly covers it – but don't make it sound too much like a private detective's brief: I went through notes on past enquiries, and when new ones came along that could possibly be related to him I brought his name into the conversations. That was almost the sum total of what I could do. What I have is a desk job, not an expanding brief.'

'I see that. But you did have some results?'

'That's putting it too definitely. I got some ideas.'

'Can you share them with me?'

'I don't see why not. There was a character, quite prominent in Jewish circles in Vienna, Salzburg, Innsbruck and so on. His name was Walter Greenspan. Round about early 1938 he faded out, but there was another man called Ludwig Weisskopf who was doing the same sort of thing.'

'And that was?'

'Getting money out of Austria and Germany so that the people he did it for had some remains of their capital when, or if, they escaped – to Britain, France (God help them!), Canada, USA and so on.'

'You got the idea that Greenspan and Weisskopf were the same person, did you?'

'Yes. I think he adopted a new identity and maybe a new appearance when things got hot for him.'

'And what did you find out, or conjecture, about him?'

'I conjectured that he worked with the Germans, which is to say the Nazis. Or, perhaps more likely, he worked with a German in an influential position.'

'That is a pretty staggering accusation.'

'Yes,' said Nora, nodding. 'Particularly on the basis of guesswork. There is more to find out – much more – than I ever proved. But what struck me was the result of all his undercover work. First of all, plenty of the people he helped – there should be inverted commas around that word if I am right – got out of Austria and made good use of the money waiting for them. The success rate – let's call it that – was rather higher than that for people who got out by their own endeavours. It needed to be, to make the business viable.'

'There's a "but" coming.'

'Yes there is. When those who got out were

ready to resume control of the part of their wealth left in Austria at the end of the war they found much of it was gone – dissipated, taken over. An even bigger "but" exists over those clients who weren't successful in getting away.'

'What's that?'

'If you go through the long list of people who got themselves involved with Mr Greenspan aka Weisskopf, there is a group who were very much richer than was generally known.'

'How did you get to know about them?'

'Because it was whispered in the Jewish community of their respective hometowns, but not known to the Aryan majority. A large number of Weisskopf's clients – let's call them that – were taken by the SS and were sent to concentration camps, where invariably they died. And here I'm talking about the late Thirties and early Forties, before the camps became mere staging posts on the road to a mass gassing.'

'In other words they were betrayed by Greenspan aka Weisskopf, who would then get a share of the proceeds?'

'Yes. That's what I think. In fairness I should say, though, that there could be other explanations: if the wealth of these people was known in the Jewish community, anyone in that community could have acted as a traitor to the individual or the community.'

'True... Two things occur to me: it seems likely this enterprise would have to be more than a one-man operation.'

'I thought of that. You're right. He would need people he could rely on to follow up rumours, if possible firm them up, check, arrange false papers and so on.'

'The other thing is, he must have been in a position of great danger himself. His German contact, the moment he felt the net closing around him, would have thrown Greenspan to the wolves. Inevitably, Greenspan would have been advertising his own position as a Jew every day of his life, unless he could use non-Jewish underlings to do the work for him. If he tried to operate mainly by telephone he was risking the distinct possibility that the line would be tapped. Most lines were.'

'You're not asking me to admire him?'

'Certainly not. But it seems a remarkable achievement if he could be proved to have survived the war.' He thought hard for a moment. 'I shall need to go to Vienna,' he said. 'There must be survivors, people who remember what was going on at the time.'

'I think you may do better by going to the States,' said Nora. 'More of them are there, if you can only get some sort of entrée.'

'But everyone there will be so far from those events. There must be some survivors in Austria, and their memories must be vivid, and revived every day as they see the place and the people.'

'There will, I suppose, be some. Indeed, I know there are. But most of the people who said Vienna was their home and they would go back to it because they had no other – most of those are dead or, quite often, have gone to Israel in an equally vain attempt to find a home. Homes are not so easily found or refound, particularly when it was that home that first cast you out and killed the remnants of your family.'

'I know it's not so easy to find a home,' said Kit.

CHAPTER THIRTEEN

One Family or the Other

Kit settled himself into the train that left
King's Cross a little after twelve. He folded
his *Times* so as to have the crossword grid and
its clues in the same segment, and then
glanced at promising-looking clues. No
revelation occurred. He remembered with a
grin his father's tetchy complaint a few weeks
before he died: 'There's new people setting
the crossword and they have no idea of the
ethics of clueing.' Kit wondered whether
people had been saying that almost from the
day, eighty-odd years before, when the stately
matron among newspapers lowered her
sights so as to take in word games. He had no
doubt that his father's death from heart
failure had not been caused by his irritation,
but perhaps it had contributed an iota to it.

He got up and went to the buffet car. The
sandwiches were the same boring choice
that had been presented to him on the train
down – maybe the same as on the train
down from Glasgow to Leeds, the first stage
of his search for his birth family. He chose
the inevitable BLT and went back to his

seat. Four people in his compartment were talking into their mobiles – conversations of the most indescribable banality which made one wonder what God's purpose in creating language had been.

Back in his seat he collected and revised his thoughts: the journey from Glasgow to Leeds had not been the opening round in his search for his birth family. That had been his mother's injunction a month or so after the specialist had delivered her death sentence. It had been on one of her bad days, and when she was lying there, her face grey against the pillow, her hand in his, she had suddenly said: 'Your mother's name and address – they're in my address book.'

The words stayed with Kit for the rest of the months remaining to his mother, though he avoided subjecting her to an inquisition. Nightmare images presented themselves of having to check out all the women's names in the book – the detritus of a busy and successful life as an art historian. Genevieve read his thoughts, and towards the end she said: 'You'll find it without any difficulty. It's in Leeds.'

Actually, Kit had been toying all those months with the idea that he might do nothing with the information that Genevieve had presented to him – might throw the address book away unopened. But that,

217

he thought, would require still more strength of mind than following up the book's information: he would be committing himself to not knowing for the rest of his natural life.

He couldn't do that. Well, he'd done all he could: located his real mother, his brothers and sister, maybe his real father too. But everything that he had found, every person from his first three years of life, told Kit about himself but left one greater mystery unsolved: why was he abducted, why was he given (sold?) to another British family? What, if any, was the connection with the Nazi persecution, then murder, of Central European Jewry?

He could not abandon the investigation where it was now. On the other hand he did not see its future progress coming from the Novello family of Pudsey, or his birth mother. The future seemed to be more with Jürgen, his adoptive – but to him always his real – father.

He gazed out at the scenery. It was flat – very flat, although it was not Norfolk. He didn't like to think of himself as the product of a flat landscape. He preferred to remember himself and his father and mother walking and motoring in the Highlands. He wondered if Jürgen had had any early memories of Bavaria and the landscapes around Munich. Holidays were probably unknown in Jürgen's early years. Holidays in the Lake District and Scotland had left Kit with happy, contented, sometimes exciting memories, and Leeds had not presented anything that illuminated his soul as the north of Scotland did – not to mention the holidays he and his parents had had in Norway and Switzerland.

Leeds, he realised, meant nothing to him.

It also, he suddenly decided as he was biting into the boring BLT sandwich, represented a false trail, or at any rate a trail that was a subsidiary part of the total mystery. And pursuing that part had led him away from the important things that really should be occupying his mind and heart. He wondered whether it was time to shuffle off Leeds and take his course in the direction of the central mystery of his early life. It would mean shuffling off some very ordinary characters: Micky, in thrall to a stronger but limited wife; Dan, an ego-mad, second-rate football player; a father who denied his paternity and whose main interest to Kit was his peculiarities.

And when he had shuffled them off, he would be taking on someone whom even now he could not quite visualise. Was he an enterprising, various, exciting figure? Or was he unadulterated evil?

His adoptive grandfather.

Kit brought into his mental gallery a

double portrait: one of his birth father, one of his adoptive father. 'Look, here on this picture and on this.' His adoptive father, Jürgen, was surrounded by an atmosphere almost entirely warm and bright – gilded by the love he and Kit had borne one another, the vivid interest each felt in the other's activities. The memories included theatre visits as well as children's Meccas such as Disneyland; it included walks too, and boat trips once his parents had found he liked them – and Genevieve had come too, even though boat trips didn't like her. The three of them did everything together if they could. And they talked about the special treats in advance, and often discussed their memories later.

And Jürgen was careful that, when Kit hit adolescence, he was left to himself as often as he liked, never forced into family activities that he was in the process of growing out of – or thought he was. If it was an upbringing that was well thought out, much premeditated, it was also spontaneous. 'Let's go and see' would be the cry of one or other of his parents and they would go and thoroughly enjoy an unplanned treat.

But what could you say of the other picture – that of his oh-so-clever birth father? Kit had had no clues as to what he might expect, and if asked in advance he would probably have said that he and his father would have to build up a relationship slowly, because they were building from almost nothing.

What he would never have guessed was that he would be totally rejected: that his father would deny that he was his son, with a ridicule of all Kit's claims that, if Kit were honest, was a response that had hurt him. His father was ironic, sarcastic, totally unmoved by emotion – at least where the conventional emotions were concerned; he was only interested in cutting down, undermining, exploding by ridicule. Kit felt for his father no more of the conventional affectionate impulses than his father felt for him.

Except that he wanted to understand him, because that could be the precondition of finding out what had happened to him, Kit, when he was three, and of understanding not just how, but why it had happened.

He wondered if a similar contrast could be drawn up if a portrait of Genevieve was placed beside a portrait of Isla. No, of course it couldn't. He was becoming fond of Isla, he felt he understood her, even to her reluctance to join him in his investigation of his abduction. She was an alternative mother, where Frank Novello was never in a million years going to be an alternative father. But as the spire of Doncaster Parish Church came into view he suddenly asked himself a question: was he beginning to love

Isla? And then another one: did he really understand her reluctance to take up again the matter of his abduction? Did she have something to hide?

He wished he could talk to his siblings without his mother being there. Can one ever be totally honest about one's parents when they are present to hear? He was willing to bet that the presence of siblings would not inhibit the Novellos. But being with their mother – the only parent to make a big contribution to their lives – had stopped a great many things being said.

When he got off the train at Leeds he went straight to one of the station's payphones, found out the number of Ada Micklejohn, then rang it. She was probably deep into one of her Barbara Cartlands but she answered immediately.

'Kit! Oh, my handsome toy boy! I got terribly mixed up last time, didn't I? Your mother and I had an awful time sorting it out. You want to see my collection again?'

'Unlike Dan, I'm not handsome, and I'm nobody's toy boy, not even yours. And I don't for the moment want to see your collection, but I am going to ask a favour of you.'

'Oh, men! They're always asking for favours, never giving them!'

'Is that a piece of Cartland wisdom? I will prove it wrong by devoting the rest of my life to finding the missing titles in your collection. I love second-hand booksellers, you see.'

'You won't find my missing titles there. They don't even acknowledge them as books. So what is the favour you want?'

'Could you ask Isla out in the next few days? It doesn't matter what it is – dinner, theatre, concert, whatever, though it would be best if it's something in the evening.'

'And what is the purpose of this invitation?' What is she being got out of the way for?'

Kit decided to confide in her.

'I think my brothers and sister would speak much more openly and candidly about the Novello family if she was not there.'

'Ah! So you want Isla out of the way so that the family can dish the dirt on her?'

'Not at all. Though if you'd said Frank instead of Isla Novello you would have been nearer the truth.'

'But Isla being there would not stop them dishing the dirt on Frank. Quite likely she would urge them on.'

'Would she? I wonder. They were married for ten or fifteen years. They must have things in common that they'd rather people did not know about. Anyway, I think it's worth a try.'

'Well, I will do it. For you, my handsome

Scottish beau, I will take her to *The Merry Widow* at the Grand. Such gorgeous melodies! You don't get such melodies from Mr Webber, do you? I don't get the same thrill from songs sung by lonely cats on the tiles. Anyway, regard it as done, my *preux chevalier* – regard her as out of the way, at least until about ten.'

Kit was received with an enthusiastic embrace by Isla, but she did not follow it up by any enquiries about what he had been doing. Isla's thoughts were taken up with the birthday of her grandchild and what she would do for her birthday if she could, but of course she wouldn't be allowed to because Pat would make all the decisions, and there wouldn't be any fun in them at all. It was all done in a resigned voice, as if she had long ago had to accept that any contest between her and her daughter-in-law had been conceded to the younger and stronger party.

'I see the ashes of a long struggle for the post of matriarch,' said Kit.

'No such thing,' said Isla. 'I wouldn't deign to struggle. And the mother was bound to win, wasn't she?'

'I'm not so sure,' said Kit. 'I've seen some pretty shameless grandparents among Jürgen and Genevieve's Scottish friends. They practically seduce the little ones.'

'What a word to use! I love them all, but I wouldn't fight over them.'

The next day, at breakfast, Isla said to Kit: 'I'm going out with Ada on Thursday. *The Merry Widow* – not really my cup of tea. I'd prefer Gilbert and Sullivan. But she was very insistent. Can you get your own dinner?'

'I think I can manage that. Or I can get someone to come out and eat with me.'

'In Leeds? You don't know anyone except family.'

Kit smiled and didn't say that wasn't true, or that family was precisely who he wanted to have dinner with. Later Isla went shopping and he phoned an Italian restaurant he'd passed that advertised a large and a small function room and booked the latter for Thursday evening. Then he rang round to Micky and Maria, getting their agreement to come to a meal, and in the case of Micky to contact Dan and pressure him and Wendy to come as well. Then he arranged a menu with La Cena Italiana and sat back thinking his morning had been well spent.

When Thursday came, the party assembled in the function room two by two, with a certain false jollity about them. Dan, of course, was last, but Wendy was suppressing all sorts of ambitious schemes and this made her much more approachable. The room was not particularly cosy but there was a welcoming smell. Since spouses had been invited there were seven in all and they drank Martinis and gin and tonics in a friendly enough fashion, apart of course from Dan, who continued expressing himself in grunts and mutterings with everyone except Kit, to whom he did not speak at all. Drink made Wendy vocal, and from one or two of her remarks Kit got the impression that Dan's ambitions to be the next Wayne Rooney-style football superstar were not going well. Wendy also made it obvious that, if this was the case, she was up for grabs.

After minestrone and before stufato genovese, Kit looked around the table and banged on a glass with a spoon. He then spoke in his normal voice, friendly, inviting, but perhaps less than warm.

'I've asked them to hold back the main course for ten minutes. There are a few things I wanted to say to you all. As you know, I've assured you that I am not interested in the family money–'

'Oh yes, you've said it,' said Dan. 'I'll believe it when I see it.'

'You can only see the money after Isla's death,' said Kit, 'and I'm sure we all hope that's a long way off. But I've asked myself, since it was not money I was after, what I did want. Why did I not only track down my birth mother's identity, but also come down to identify myself to her, and meet you all?

And I'm sure that the obvious answer is the right one: I wanted to have a family again – including people of my own age, something I'd never had in the past.'

'I think everyone understands that,' said Micky. 'And I think we've welcomed you.'

'You have, most of you. But there's been the shadow of a barrier between us. Dan here exemplifies it most obviously. That barrier means there are some doubts: if I'm really who I claim to be; if I'm on the make, whoever I am; if the family actually wants a new member.'

'I certainly do,' said Maria.

'Thank you. But the fact remains: because I wanted to find a family, I assumed I would be welcomed by people pleased to have been found. But why should I be? All you three children of Isla and Frank grew up as a family. You all knew there was one brother who had been taken from you. You knew that Isla grieved for him and always would do. But you could not grieve for someone you barely remembered, if at all. The family unit did not include me, and though relationships and interest would always be polite, they would never be close or passionate.'

'Where exactly is this heading?' asked Pat.

'Fair point. The point I think is that I'm saying I was a fool to think I could fit into a family unit that had been complete for so long without me. I hope we see each other when I come down to see Isla, but I doubt I will ever be more than a "friend of the family".'

'If that,' said Dan.

'If that,' Kit agreed. 'Now, the other thing I want to say follows from that. If we are not going to be close in the future, I need to know from you now anything that may have a bearing on what happened in Sicily all those years ago. There may be things so trivial you haven't thought to mention them, or it may be they didn't seem to reflect well on us as a family. Either way, please tell me now, or in the next day or two while I'm still in Leeds. Let me add whatever information you have to my little store of clues and indications – things that may eventually lead somewhere or may not.' They all looked at him, some with calculation in their eyes. 'Agreed?'

They nodded.

'When shall we talk about this?' asked Micky.

'At the end of the meal – ah, here's the main course.'

It was much later, after spoons were being laid aside from the inevitable *dolce*, and while Dan was licking his with an enthusiasm that suggested dieting was never going to be part of his regimen, that Kit once again looked around the table and said: 'Well?'

From her position at the other end of the table Maria raised a finger.

'Just one thing – one tiny little thing. I was having a good old confab the other day with Pat's Auntie Flora–'

'You know her well?'

'Ah ... you probably don't realise: Micky and Pat have been going together since primary school. Pat used to come round and help him with his homework. All our family do's included members of her family and vice versa – so yes, I do know her well, and she's the best gossip of all of us.'

'Just what we need,' said Kit.

'And Auntie Flora said that Mother – Isla – was always desperately in love with Dad. It's not the impression she likes to give now. She suggests – even if it's only by tone of voice – that the marriage went very flat and was destroyed by the kidnapping, and that she's now totally disillusioned with Dad, which may well be true. But she was always, when Flora came to know her, besotted with him, completely under his thumb, and not in any way discontented with her lot. The sun shone out of his ... you know. We children probably just accepted it as the natural order of things, but in fact that sort of subservience in marriage had been out of fashion for decades.'

'I think I caught some of that,' said Micky. 'Being the eldest, I was a bit bewildered.

Other kids' parents were not like that – Pat's weren't for a start. In our household Frank was the big panjandrum whose every wish had to be obeyed and whose comfort was everybody's first priority. I didn't notice any major change at the time of the kidnap, but of course, the disappearance of one of us children was what was on our minds for months afterwards.'

'Interesting,' said Kit.

'One additional piece of info,' said Ivor Battersby, stretching his long legs under the dining table. 'I was dining with the Rotary Club the other night, and I was placed next to a solicitor. The talk came round to my father-in-law... Well, the fact is, I brought it round. This solicitor had known him well. Said that in his time Frank was a first-rate legal brain: cautious, reliable even when he was dealing with hot potatoes like the Glasgow gang wars, which he got into because of his Italian background. He agreed that there was no great change in him at the time of the abduction and divorce. He set himself up in a posh flat near St Paul's Square, had a succession of girl-friends – not usually live-in ones, had a good life to all intents and purposes. The change came later.'

'Micky could add something to that,' said Pat.

If Micky could have thrown his wife

glances that could kill, he would have done so. Instead he just swallowed.

'Yes, well... I don't know. I normally make a fool of myself when I have to speak in public. Remember when I was your best man, Ivor?'

'You did very well,' his brother-in-law said. 'You are the only one who doesn't think so.'

'Try and talk as if we were speaking to each other alone after dinner,' said Kit.

'I don't think that that would make any difference. You're an educated man – I'm just a man with a roller and a tin of paint. Oh well, here goes.'

He swallowed, looking at Kit, then started.

'You all know I've seen Dad on and off since the divorce. For a time – not long – he saw us kids: not often, but still, regularly, maybe every three or four months. I didn't notice much difference in him then, and not for long afterwards. I knew in my heart that these were duty occasions and no pleasure to him at all, but still... When they ceased Maria and Dan were pleased, but I wanted them to go on.'

'Why?' asked Kit.

'Because I thought they ought to go on, I suppose. It's what happens when parents divorce. I always like to do the done thing, the ordinary thing. So I rang him and said could I come and see him. He must have thought word would get around if he said "no". So generally we met up, though it was never a pleasure for either of us. Then things started to change.'

'In what way?'

'In the past he'd always been the correct, buttoned-up solicitor, running to type, I suppose. We generally went to sporting events, though I'd have liked a bit more variety. And he started saying things that seemed ... well, wrong for him, as I'd always known him. One day at a rugby league match, he introduced me to one of his clients, and he said: "This is my boy, Micky. He's a good lad. Never wanted to go to university. Saved me a mint of money that has." Do you see why I was surprised?'

'I think so,' said Kit. 'It was thoughtless, cynical, slightly "off". It showed he didn't care how he hurt you, didn't care about your feelings at all.'

'That's it. And I'd always wanted to be important to him. I was hurt, very hurt.'

'Were the remarks always aimed at you?'

'Oh, not at all. Sometimes the family perhaps, sometimes just general remarks. They were always things that a solicitor, a good one, wouldn't say. And he said them, and enjoyed saying them.'

'And this has gone on, has it?'

'Oh yes. I went to see him the other day, and he asked me if I'd seen Isla's by-blow recently. It's as if he's losing all his inhibitions and natural cautions and now flaunts what he once would have shrunk from saying.'

'What precipitated his going into a nursing home?'

'A broken leg. And he found he preferred being looked after, and decided to stay there.'

'Ah. No reason there for a change of mood and character. I wondered because what happens to a lot of people with Alzheimer's and other diseases of the elderly is that they seem to change their whole nature, whereas in fact it is long-hidden things emerging and making them seem transformed. I'm sure you know the sort of thing: elderly spinsters with a command of four-letter words that family and friends find astonishing.'

'Ah yes, I've heard of that sort of case,' said Micky. 'There was another odd occasion recently – not like that, but interesting. Often he's quite quiet when we get together – whether it's in his bedroom at the nursing home or at a home game at Elland Road – and he sometimes makes odd remarks that come from what he has been thinking in the long periods of silence. Ten days ago we were at the football game, and a goal had just been scored by Leeds, and suddenly he said: "They said it could be slow, but I never thought it would be as slow as this."

They all looked at each other. Dan's eyes revealed a mind that was struggling with new information.

'That sounds like a death sentence,' he said finally. And we're the only family he's got...' he looked around the room, 'we three.'

'I don't think that's how Micky reads the remark,' said Kit, in a low voice. 'And he's the one who was there.' Micky nodded.

'That's right. I read it that he'd been told a while ago that he was in the early stages of Alzheimer's, or maybe senility. I believe those are pretty unpredictable illnesses to get, so far as the rate of their progress and so on are concerned. I read it that he was expressing surprise that he – and his brain – had been so long in developing the illness.'

'I think that's how I read it,' said Kit.

Suddenly Maria changed the tack of the meeting.

'To go back to what Micky quoted earlier,' she said, 'that about Isla's by-blow. Wouldn't it make more sense, if Isla did produce a child that wasn't her husband's, that that child would be Dan rather than Peter – sorry – Kit?'

'How do you work that out?' asked Pat, though it was through gargled outrage and 'what the hells?' from Dan.

'I'm just thinking of the usual pattern of a disintegrating marriage: it makes sense if

234

Kit was unwanted by his father at least, and if Isla responded with a protest – the opposite of her earlier worship of him. If Frank went elsewhere – and he clearly had a line-up of girlfriends after the divorce, which suggests a straying eye all through the marriage – then maybe Isla felt: if he can, why shouldn't I?'

'Yes, I see that,' said Ivor Battersby. 'The alternative is that this marriage disintegrated earlier than most people realised; ignoring Auntie Flora – though in my experience she is usually right – and Kit was the result of an affair, what does that imply about Dan? You might ask: why did he come into the world at all?'

'A lot of us have often wondered,' said Maria.

'Here, I'm not sitting through garbage like that,' yelled Dan as if he was being accused of a blatant foul. 'If I was conceived when the marriage was on the rocks it was because Dad was careless like we all are at times. I'm going.'

And he threw his chair back against the wall and marched out of the function room, followed reluctantly, with wistful glances at Kit, by Wendy.

'Not so much careless as brainless,' she muttered to whoever was in earshot.

'Well, that's given us plenty to think about,' said Kit, realising that, whether he wanted it to or not, the meeting was drawing to a close.

Kit was conscious of a chill in the air from the moment he awoke next morning.

'Tea,' said his mother, putting it down with a clang beside his bed and going straight out.

She had already gone to bed by the time he had arrived back in Seldon Road the night before. Kit went straight up to bed himself, with more than enough to think about. But 'tea', without a comment on the weather or cheery chaffing on his sleeping late, did give him a clue to her mood. He washed and showered in a hurry and went downstairs. Mail was lying in a bundle on the hall table, secured by the inevitable red elastic band. He quickly sorted through it and left his in a separate pile. Then he went into the dining room.

'Lovely day,' he said to Isla.

'Is it? I haven't had time to notice. I presume you want cereal?' she said in a sour tone. She didn't say anything about the eggs and bacon and sausages which he did not want but which she slapped down in front of him before going out. He felt obliged to eat as much as he could, and then a bit more.

'Toast and marmalade,' Isla said, coming in the moment he put his knife and fork together on the plate.

'Best part of the meal,' said Kit. 'Now, are you going to tell me what this is all about?'

'I don't know what you mean,' she said, going out. Kit buttered and marmaladed a slice of toast, then went in a casual fashion, plate in hand, and stood in the doorway to the kitchen.

'What "this is about",' he said, 'is the ice in your manner. You're about as welcoming as a winter congregation of Wee Frees. I've done something that has annoyed or offended you – right?'

She turned round, her hands on her hips.

'There's no "or" – I'm both... Ada Micklejohn drove me home last night after the opera. We went along Bennett Street, just as practically my whole family came rolling out of La Cena Italiana. If you'd asked me, I could have told you of a much better restaurant than that. But of course, you didn't ask me, did you?'

'No, I didn't.'

'So I was humiliated in front of Ada, who'd asked where you were eating and I'd said you were having a pub meal with your brother Micky.'

'I don't see anything very humiliating in a change of plan.'

'It was not a change of plan. I know all of Ada's little Mills & Boon affectations. You persuaded her to ask me out to give you a clear field with the rest of the family.'

Kit sighed.

'OK. But it wasn't so much a clear field I wanted. I didn't want to bully or manipulate them in any way. I just wanted to test them, to see if there were any memories they'd suppressed, or hadn't spoken of because they thought they might offend or upset you, so that they would have kept quiet about anything that reflected badly on the family.'

'You wanted to drag up anything that reflected badly on the family,' said Isla, her voice overflowing with bitterness. 'I've always tried to show the best possible face to the world, and I tried to make Micky and Maria do the same.'

'Not Dan, I notice,' said Kit, going into the hall. 'You love him, but you recognise he's a lost cause.' He riffled through his mail and then looked at Isla. 'There was a letter from Vienna when I sorted through my mail. What have you done with it?'

'I don't know what you're talking about.'

Kit shook his head.

'Oh dear, Mother. You've ruled the roost too long. You haven't got together a little collection of denials and excuses or counter-accusations. Of course you've taken it. Who else could have done it? We're alone in the house. In fact, I think I can see the outline of an envelope in the pocket of your apron. Let me have it.'

As he walked towards her she took it from the pocket and threw it on the floor.

'There it is. Take it. You know I've always hated you going into these matters from the past.'

'That doesn't excuse theft.' He slit open the envelope and took out a single sheet. He cast his eye over the content. 'I have been informed by the Austrian embassy in London ... my old friend Mrs Madison ... I am an old man with an old man's fallible memory ... if you would care to pay me a visit I will tell you what I know and what I suspect ... I regard it as your right to be told ... Helmut Erheim.'

Kit looked at Isla, who suddenly seemed to cast a threatening shadow. She was staring at the letter, her face drained of blood.

'This is a letter about things connected with my adoptive grandfather. I don't see how it in any way concerns you or why you should object to my following it up.'

'You would take no notice of my objections in any case.'

'That's true. I think since I'm doing something that upsets you it would be as well if I moved out of the house.'

'Please yourself,' said Isla Novello.

Ten minutes later Kit had packed the two changes of clothes he had with him, the Marks & Sparks underwear and the big Victorian novel that he had been reading since the day he had first walked up Seldon Road in search of number 35. It was not a very lavish collection of possessions. Perhaps he had suspected from the start that the answer to his fundamental question was not here, or was only partly to be found in the Novello family. He was surprised to discover that he could leave the Novellos without much thought of coming back.

CHAPTER FOURTEEN

The Errand Boy

Kit walked around the wide, open spaces of Vienna, wishing he had Genevieve and her artistic sensitivity with him to point out half-hidden beauties and assertions of a power now long since crumbled. His appointment with Helmut Erheim was for half past twelve, and from time to time he stopped for a coffee or a fruit juice, often opening the man's letter to see if he had missed any points of interest. The handwriting was difficult, but the hand that had written it was firm and confident.

Dear Mr Philipson,
I have been informed by the Austrian embassy in London that you are interested in finding out about the life and career of the late Walter Greenspan. It was my old friend Mrs Madison who contacted me, and it is certainly a fascinating subject – his career was as interesting and varied as the number of pseudonyms he went under. I would be delighted to talk to you.
Please remember I am an old man with an old man's fallible memory, and the time when I

knew this man was a tumultuous one in which much may have got jumbled together in the memory of a player in that national tragedy. If you would care to pay me a visit I will tell you what I know and what I suspect, but you must not give absolute trust to all the details of what I tell you. The broad thrust, however, will be true and clear. I regard it as your right to be told, and I will tell it without sensationalism or self-righteousness. Remember I was for a time involved with the things Greenspan did, and I was therefore, though in small ways, contaminated by them.

I look forward to meeting you.

Helmut Erheim.

Kit folded up the letter and put it back in his pocket. Then he downed the dregs of his coffee and stood up. The April sunshine was weak, but pleasantly so, and he walked in the direction of the synagogue and the old Jewish Museum, now amalgamated and closed, with all its memories, mostly bad, distributed elsewhere. Finally, he made his way to the house in which Herr Erheim lived.

When he found it, he stood for a moment on the little step outside and tried to prepare himself. But how can you prepare yourself for something you have no knowledge of or presentiment about? Of the man he was going to meet he knew nothing, or next to nothing. So he had to be ready for uncertainty, and for an uncertainty that would remain after the interview if, as the letter had warned, he could not put total credence in the testimony. He put his finger on the bell and rang it.

The response was very quick. He had been waited for, maybe even looked for. Did he appear so English that he could be picked out from the native Viennese throng? Bolts were pulled on the other side of the door and it opened confidently. Waiting to welcome him, smiling and making a little bob, was a square-shouldered woman in her early thirties, in a white blouse and lavish black skirt with large embroidered flowers. A warm, optimistic, friendly person.

'Welcome to Vienna, Herr Philipson! Herr Erheim is expecting you and is looking forward to your talk.'

She stood aside and he came into a tiny square hallway at the bottom of a wooden staircase.

'Thank you,' murmured Kit. 'Is it up?' The woman laughed.

'The only way is up.'

'Difficult for an old man to negotiate,' commented Kit.

'Negotiate?'

'To cope with. To climb up.'

'Oh, Grandad rarely leaves his flat these days. If he ever does there are attendants who help him down in a wheelchair. He does not enjoy that. To tell you the truth he loves his apartment and would rather not leave it.'

'I can understand that. He is your grandfather, you say?'

'Great-grandfather in fact, but that is a mouthful to say over and over again. I am his nurse, pupil, companion. Everything possible. I love him very much and always have. I am studying World Literature at Vienna University, so it is very convenient. I live with Grandad and do all I can for him, and study as well.' They paused at the first floor, swallowed, then mounted the next flight of wooden stairway.

'Last one. He has the whole of what you English would call the second floor. We call it the third floor. It used to be the museum curator's. He is very comfortable here. All his friends make sure of that.' She opened the door. 'Grandpapa – here is your English visitor!'

The room was a substantial one, obviously the flat's living room, which had gained a large bed to accommodate the old man; it was facing the door, and the old man sat up in the bed, royally genial and welcoming, wearing a dressing gown and a woollen hat that made him look like a Dickens illustration. There was apparently pleasure and welcome in his smiles and gestures, but behind these, Kit suspected, also a certain cunning and a pleasure in combat. Perhaps he saw Kit's visit as a challenge.

'So you have come to Vienna especially to see me. I am flattered, but I'm unsure precisely what you want of me. Heidi – a tray for Mr ... er ... Philipson, and one for me. A simple lunch, my dear boy, but you must have a glass of wine with it. I am forbidden wine by my doctor, so I will have one too. Austrian wine is ridiculously underrated.'

Heidi fetched a bottle already opened from the little kitchen area and poured for them both large and well-filled glasses. Though he was not hungry, Kit tucked into the cold meats and salad on the little tray that Heidi had put on his knee. She came back from the kitchen with a light coat on. Her grandfather looked at her with pride.

'That's right, Heidi. Go to your lectures. If I could have gone to lectures when I was a youngster then perhaps I would have been a better man... Or there again, perhaps not.' When Heidi had closed the door behind her Erheim, grinning conspiratorially, added: 'Now, while you are eating you must tell me about yourself, and when we have finished the repast and the bottle I will tell you what I know about Walter Greenspan, and what my connection with him was. Is that agreed?'

Kit nodded, but this was something he

had not expected. He cleared his throat nervously.

'I was brought up in Glasgow by my adoptive parents. My mother was a university lecturer in the Faculty of Fine Arts, and my father was a deputy editor on one of the Glasgow daily papers. We were a close, happy family.'

'A very literate, professional family, is that right?'

'Very much so. But not too solemn.'

'But these, you say, were not your real parents?'

'That's not how I would put it ... but no. As I told you in my letter in response to yours, I had a few very shadowy memories of the first three years of my life. I suspected that perhaps my real mother had died. But, as I say, I was happy with my adoptive parents – what I call in my mind my real parents – so I didn't enquire in case it was a painful matter for them. In fact, over the years, I'm afraid I forgot my memories of anything else.' Herr Erheim nodded.

'Things began to change when my father fell ill. The main thing I knew about his early life was that he was one of the Kindertransport – the children who got out of Germany just before the war started.'

'You don't need to fill in the background for me. I lived through it.'

'Of course. Well, he was one of the last out,

246

and was always grateful for that – and perhaps a bit guilty-feeling towards all those who didn't get out.'

'The dead children. Yes, I can understand that. And the name he went under – was it Jürgen Greenspan?'

'"Went under"? I don't understand... You know, I never asked about his and Hilda's surname before they were adopted by the Philipsons.'

'Never mind,' said Erheim, with a wave of the hand putting the matter aside. 'I think I once met your father, though of course, that was when he was so young there is little to be said about him. Quiet and serious, I'd guess.'

'Yes. He remained that. I think that while he was ill he must have persuaded Genevieve to come clean with me over the "adoption' – give me all the facts. He must have thought it was well time. But my mother was diagnosed as having late-stage breast cancer not very long after his death, and so we never had the in-depth session. We talked about it but she was too weak for scenes. She only directed me towards her address book, and told me my birth mother was named Novello. I had vague memories of an earlier family and a strange plane trip, so I checked the old newspaper files and discovered I'd been abducted.'

'And that is what you've been investigating

since, is it?'

'Yes.'

Unsure of what should be the correct reaction to an announcement of a childhood abduction, Herr Erheim waved his eloquent hand in the direction of the bottle.

'Have another glass of this not entirely despicable wine...'

'It's very good. But I'm no expert...'

Herr Erheim bowed his thanks.

'Now let me tell you how I came to meet the man who interests you, and what I came to know.' He settled back comfortably against his pillows. 'The first meeting came in 1932.'

'So early? Before Jürgen's birth.'

'Exactly. And before the Nazi takeover of this once-great country of Austria. I was only half Austrian – my mother's side – and I grew up mainly in Germany, but I have a peculiar tenderness for this country and its capital. In that year, 1932, I was twelve, and I was in Berlin rather loosely boarding with an uncle of mine. The economic situation was appalling, and I organised a little band of child musicians who went around the bars and the clubs of the capital in the early evening – before their own entertainment started, and early enough for us not to be told we ought to be in bed. We had boys and girls in this band, and we played New Orleans stuff, stuff from the latest musicals –

Showboat, No, No Nanette and so on – and though I say it myself we were quite good. I was the organiser, the clarinet player and the master of ceremonies. It must have been in that last role that I caught Greenspan's eye. It was in the Hofmeister Bar, and when we were leaving after the collection had been taken he beckoned me over. "Very good," he said. "You're a promising lad. Here's my card. If you're ever in Vienna or Frankfurt the card has my contact numbers there. I'll find something for you to do. A lad like you deserves a better life than glorified begging. Now remember, and keep this card. There's bad times coming for us Jews.'"

Kit seemed to see in the man's face a shadow of the surprise the young Erheim must have felt.

'Was this news to you?'

'Completely. Both that the Jews had a bad time coming, and that I could be identified with "the Jews". Of course, I knew I was Jewish, but thought that that was no more important than that some Germans were Prussians, some were Bavarians. So what, I'd always felt? Well, in the years that followed I learnt what it meant to be a Jew, and it was nothing like being a Prussian.'

'Hadn't you read newspapers?'

'What boy of twelve reads newspapers? Then, in the summer of 1936, I went with a young English writer to Vienna. It was

249

wonderful – a dream city – the buildings, the landscape, the mountains. I won't tell you what the English boy and I got up to. We played, we quarrelled, we made up. I quite enjoyed the quarrels but I didn't really enjoy the makings up. I'd taken that card with me. One day when we'd had an almighty row I rang the number, spoke to Greenspan, then went to see him. The English boy went back to Berlin. I stayed on working for my new benefactor.'

'What were you doing?'

Erheim looked at Kit, but blinked. He seemed uncertain whether to boast or apologise about his activities.

'Getting people and their money out of the country.'

'Yes, I'd heard hints of that. By "people" you mean Jews, I suppose.'

'Yes, almost entirely – just one or two Gentiles who'd fallen foul of the German or Austrian governments. We got rich Jews out, also their children, their mistresses. We ran a superb business – he ran, I should say. I was just the messenger boy.'

'What did the "messenger boy" do?'

'Delivered tickets, collected inordinate fees for services rendered ... and quite a lot of stuff for Mr Greenspan himself.' He winked. He'd decided to be brazen.

'Personal stuff?'

'Women?'

'Yes, oh yes, women. It was when I was doing personal stuff that I saw the boy who I think became your father.'

'You visited the family?'

'Yes. You've heard of the mother?

'I read a bit of a diary written by Jürgen's sister, Hilde. There were mentions of the mother. Hilde's view of her was in a way contradictory, but she obviously thought her mother was being unfair to her husband in many of the things she said about him to the children.'

Erheim, after trying to suppress his reaction, burst out into a howl of laughter.

'Unfair? Oh dear me, what a sad joke! The woman was obsessed with him. He could do anything and be forgiven. How do you think Jürgen came into the world, years after his sister, except as a result of a session of "forgiveness"? Oh dear – women don't come more wrong-headed than Elisabeth Greenspan, as she called herself. When he was away from her, which was almost all the time, she could judge him justly. As soon as he reappeared, she went weak at the knees. I thought it was strange that Walter Greenspan told me all this, but I think it was a kind of boasting.'

'You say "as she called herself". Was Elisabeth not married to him?'

Erheim's face twisted in ridicule.

'She had gone through a ceremony which

had no legal validity at all. I think Walter Greenspan had got some of his actor friends to put something together that might fox her. He rejoiced in her naivety. The only thing he ever did to oblige her, getting the children on board that train, was, I thought, a little word of thanks for the joy that her artlessness had given him over the years.'

'Sad, sad,' said Kit. 'What happened to her?'

Erheim shrugged.

'What happened to Jews in Central Europe? She was no different from the rest. Enough of her, young man. She was not important.'

Kit was for a moment speechless. It was the man's first big mistake, the moment when the curtains briefly collapsed, showing the cynical hardness Erheim would surely conceal from most of his visitors.

'I would guess that that fate didn't overtake Walter Greenspan,' Kit said. His voice held no note of condemnation, and Erheim's reply showed no sign of his having registered any disapproval.

'Not on your life! Too sharp, too intelligent, and blessed with contacts everywhere, including the Gestapo and the SS. Not that things weren't – what's that funny word you have? – hairy now and then. I was still employed by him and running his errands in 1941. I was in greater danger than him of getting caught, but I would only be a small cog in the wheel, so where he, if he'd been caught, would have been shot or something worse and slower, I would have been sent to one of the camps, which were then not quite the murder factories they later became.'

'I suppose you decided to get out. You knew all the best ways.'

'Of course I did. Turkey was one of the best routes out. I was having papers forged for a rich Viennese Jew's son. I pocketed the papers, put my photograph on, and took the route through Romania. The government there was Fascist, anti-Semitic, but the king was biding his time and the country was yearning to change sides. I had a lot of help and I got through to Turkey, and stayed there till Greece was liberated.'

'And the rich Jew's son?'

Erheim's shrivelled shoulders were shrugged again.

'How would I know? The fate of Central Europe's Jews. Don't ask me such questions. If you were a Jew at that time you could not afford a delicate conscience.'

And Kit had to agree that that was probably true. He had not experienced the horror. Perhaps he should not judge. As Erheim said nothing, seemingly lost in reminiscence, he asked: 'Do you remember the Greenspan children on the day of the Kindertransport?'

'Do I remember? Of course. I was there. My benefactor sent me to Frankfurt to meet them.' He frowned trying to recall details. 'I managed to get them moved from a train on September 5th to one on the 29th of August. I sensed that war would come quickly and I wanted to get back as soon as possible to Vienna. Hitler was desperate for war. The children got out just in time. I saw them kissing their mother goodbye on a miserable field near the station, where no one would see them except other children, other parents. They hated sympathy, the Nazis, and they feared that family scenes like that would arouse it.'

'And the later train never went, I suppose?'

'No. The outbreak of war put a stop to it. All the children booked on it died. Hilde and Jürgen got through. They had a little pile of money which I brought them from their father. He was always generous.'

'To himself as well, I've heard. It's said he sometimes took clients' money and sent them to their deaths.'

'I never knew of anything of that sort,' said Erheim, firing up. 'I was a very straight boy, and he only involved me in above-board transactions – in so far as anything could be "above board" in Nazi Germany and Austria. That was the reason I split up from him and decamped to Turkey. It was a feeling that the Gestapo was getting close and they would take me just for being Jewish.'

'How did you know they were getting close?'

'Greenspan talked about it the last time we met. He was preparing to get out of Austria too. His main contact in the SS was going to help him. The SS man felt safer with Greenspan out of the country.'

'He didn't go to Turkey, I suppose – or you would know more about what happened to him.'

'I know enough, boy,' said Erheim wryly. 'But no, he didn't. It was one of his few miscalculations. He had got people out through Italy before. It was the least policed of the borders because the new Nazi rulers of Austria calculated that escapees wouldn't want to go from one Fascist country to another.'

'Why would they?'

'Because Greenspan – and he was not alone – took the view that Mussolini didn't care a fig if a man was a Jew or a Pole or a Czech. He only persecuted a few Italian Jewish families to convince Hitler that he was with him on the racial question. In fact, his only interest in Jews was to squeeze money out of them. If they had money they could buy immunity in Italy. It was Greenspan's view that he would be safe as long as he could stump up, and this, I heard later, he did for his first few months there.'

'Where was he living?'

'Venice, after he'd taken the train there with forged papers all in order. By then the fortunes of war, as they called them, were changing. The Allies were invading Sicily. By the time they got to the mainland Greenspan had moved south hoping to change sides, and was almost in the firing line. He was arrested and imprisoned in the nearest Italy had at that date to a concentration camp.'

'Where was that?'

'Ferramonti, on the mainland, in Calabria, not far from Naples. He'd gone south hoping to get to the Allied part of southern Italy because he saw them as the inevitable victors. By then camps for Jews had been set up all over Italy. Eventually most of the inmates were transported to Auschwitz and other camps.'

'It doesn't sound as if Mussolini was an unenthusiastic anti-Semite.'

'At that point his whole hold on power – what little he had – depended on the German troops. He would have liked to go on squeezing the Jews rather than imprisoning them, but he had no choice. Soon he was retreating northwards with the German army.'

'How did you find out all this?'

'When Greenspan vanished from Vienna I

was still working for him, and I had, as my final task, to get a young Jewish man out of Austria and into Italy. When we met last I told him to write to me in coded terms if he had any news of Greenspan. In Istanbul I went to the British embassy every day to read reliable newspapers in their reading room. It was then that I perfected my English. They kept mail for people they knew, whether English or not. The young man sent me a letter with hints about Greenspan, whom he called Durataverdi – the nearest he could get to Greenspan in Italian. He'd been in Venice, had come south, and was by then in Ferramonti, the Calabrian camp, with Gypsies, Mafiosi and homosexuals, showing that Mussolini was definitely dancing to Hitler's tunes. As the war was drawing to a close I wrote a letter to Signor Durataverdi in Ferramonti and sent another version to the Eighth Army. I never had any reply.'

Kit tried to digest the sad little story.

And that was the end of your relationship with Greenspan?'

'It was, strictly speaking. But something happened later, much later, that made me think. I can't put an exact date to it. Let's say 1995 for an approximation. By then Greenspan would have been in his eighties. It was a time when the Italian government was engaged in a big closedown of the Mafia and related societies. This happens periodically in Italy, or rather does not happen because it's mostly talk and nothing gets done. This time more was done, many were arrested, one of the judges who was drafted in to ensure that something was done was killed and another lost his bottle – lovely phrase – and fled from south Italy, or the Mezzogiorno as the Italians call it. The difficulty was in getting convictions, as with all gangland crimes. One after another of the accused men were acquitted. One of the men mentioned in the news accounts – I expect you could guess – had the name–'

'Durataverdi. A distinctive name. Then you must have learnt a lot about him from the newspapers, and I could do the same.'

'I don't think you'll learn as much as you think. I certainly did what you say, read all the papers I could get hold of, but the fact that he was acquitted did not help. It made editors scared of libel actions. Then there was the fact that he was apparently a bit of a man of mystery, even with his fellow crooks. References to his origins often used vague forms like "Eastern European" or "shrouded in mystery". Only one account of him mentioned Austria or Vienna as his place of origin, and I'm not sure that was correct: his accent when I knew him was Central German. Later it was varied, depending where he was. The only fact that one of the journalists had, which then spread to all the other newspapers, was that Durataverdi had been imprisoned in the notorious Ferramonti concentration camp during the war. That fact enabled other ex-inmates to earn a few thousand lire by peddling to the papers their memories of the place. There were few memories of Greenspan, probably due to the usual fear of reprisals. There's no doubt in my mind that he was pretty high up in the Mafia hierarchy. And that he was the man I knew here in Vienna so long ago. No doubt either that he squirmed his way into the organis-ation while he was in Ferramonti ... and that, my dear young fellow, is all I know about the man who may or may not be your adoptive grandfather, if such a relationship exists. Let us share the rest of the wine.'

Kit shook his head.

'Not for me, thank you. I want to keep my head clear.'

'There are some subjects for which it is better not to have a clear head. I will there-fore take on the task of drinking to the bottom of the bottle. Death to doctors!'

He was clearly in a high-spirited mood, perhaps with having told all he knew about Greenspan. He drank with relish. Though he must have hidden many aspects of himself from his admiring visitors over the years, he didn't bother to hide his relish for food and drink. Very Austrian!

'So Greenspan was never legally married to Elisabeth Greenspan?'

Erheim indulged in one of his raucous laughs.

'Of course not! Never! And never to anyone else, in the time I knew him, though with some others he may also have had some theatrical version of the ceremony. Why do you ask? Is it important to you to find out there was a marriage? Would the lack of it have worried Jürgen or Genevieve?'

'I don't think so. After all, I suspect they adopted me thinking I was the illegitimate offspring of a respectable English or Scottish family.'

'Was that how you were "sold" to him and his wife?'

'Something of the kind. I feel sure they never knew I was abducted.'

'Abducted, eh? Maybe that would have worried Jürgen.'

'I'm sure it would. He was a worrier because he was a man of conscience. He worried because he was a survivor when almost all his fellow German-Jewish children were gassed. He worried about many of the things done by the state of Israel. So he would have worried if he had learnt – and I think he did learn, in a nasty encounter with my birth father – how he and Genevieve came to be my parents by believing a lie, credible though that lie was.'

'Rest his bones,' said Erheim, with the touch of cynicism in his voice that had by now become endemic. 'I don't know what worriers do in Heaven, if it exists. Now I must have my afternoon nap – my siesta. I have another visitor tonight... You know, I have many visitors, mostly Austrian or German people by origin, anxious to know the fates of their ancestors or relatives. I tell them, most of them, that I know nothing about their relative, but the likelihood is they suffered the common fate of European Jews. I say it more gently than I said it to you. But you know, I have never before been asked about Walter Greenspan. You are the first. And who knows how many offspring he left behind him, eh?'

He raised his hand and dismissed Kit by turning over to sleep. Kit scuttled out of the bedroom-cum-sitting room and scrambled down the ill-lit wooden staircase. At the door he met Heidi coming in, and thanked her for her hospitality. 'Lecture cancelled?' he asked.

'No, I am between lectures. In my preparations to receive you I forgot a book I need this afternoon.'

'Why should you make preparations to receive me? I'm nobody.'

'You were unusual. You were asking about Mr Greenspan, and nobody's ever done that since I came to live with Grandad.'

'He just commented on that, and added it was surprising since he had so many illegitimate children.'

'Perhaps they are all dead, and their mothers too. If so, he did not help them escape, when he could have done that more easily than most. But he is one who comes into many of the stories that Grandad often tells. Mostly people come to see him because they admire his wonderful work to get Jews out of Nazi Austria. And Greenspan had his part in that, that I have heard often. Grandad has been awarded the Austria Medal for all he did. He likes to talk to people about it, and he's always very modest. He was one of many, he says, but I'm not sure he was. He never mentions any particular people. Maybe he was almost alone. His life proves that the individual can make a great difference, don't you agree?'

'An individual can certainly change history,' said Kit, trying hard not to sound too careful, but unwilling to agree to the first part of her last sentence.

As he walked back to his hotel, he tried to put his thoughts in order. He wondered whether Erheim's association with Greenspan was as virtuous as he, in the early part of the talk, tried to portray it. Would Greenspan have chosen such a scruple-ridden assistant, even if his function was no more than to be the messenger boy? It was surely much more likely that Erheim knew he was on to a good thing financially, and was employed by Greenspan on terms that gave him a proportion of the profits.

Erheim the man seemed to take delight in giving glancing hints at the true nature of the personality and actions of the national hero he had become. He seemed underneath to be the archetypal 'wide boy', with his eye on the main chance.

Austria had hidden its complicity with its Nazi masters by papering over Erheim's true motives and transforming him into a hero fit to be worshipped by the international liberal intelligentsia.

No one had ever done a similar service for Walter Greenspan. Kit was desperately keen to find out why.

CHAPTER FIFTEEN

Progenitor

The Mafia, it seemed, was a growth industry. When Kit got back to Glasgow he investigated the public libraries and then the chain bookshops; many books, some of them fat, confidently awaited borrowers and buyers. He conjectured that it was the burgeoning of offshoots of organised crime on the parent tree in Bulgaria and several ex-Soviet states that had renewed interest. Or perhaps the endless *Godfather* film sequence back in the last century still fetched in aficionados who could not get enough assassinations and double-crossings. The books divided themselves into tomes written by academics (sometimes so opaque in style as to need a translator) and tomes written by journalists (whose English style suggested a continual state of hysteria or apoplexy). He borrowed the academic tome that seemed most approachable and the journalistic tome that seemed to state its sources when it was safe to do so. He snatched a quick and safe meal from the freezer and settled down to a good, if lengthy, read.

Surprisingly, he had got into the habit of ringing Isla in Pudsey every two or three evenings. He found it difficult to define why he was doing this because the relationship remained, for the moment, a tense one. He decided he must have retreated to that atavistic feeling: after all, she is ... and so on. He felt rather surprised that he did react this way at all, with all the accompanying burden of feeling traitorous to Genevieve. It was now three days since he had rung Leeds, but he failed to remember that he should.

There was no mention in either of his books of anyone called Durataverdi.

He did not feel that this was in any way a disproof of Erheim's conviction that Greenspan had ended up as a top Mafia boss. Authors had to be careful. Erheim had mentioned that at the time of the trial Durataverdi was still alive, and could therefore bring libel actions if he was found not guilty. In both books the handling of the anti-Mafia drive was sketchy, presumably for the same reasons.

The author of the more academic of the two books, Richard Marston, was a senior lecturer in the Department of Italian Studies at London's City University. Kit rang the university six times before he got on to his man, so busy was he spreading news of Italian culture to the young of the capital.

'Could I have five minutes of your time?'

Kit began.

'I could maybe manage seven,' came the reply. He sounded young, even if, with such a massive volume to his name, he probably wasn't.

'My name is, or rather was, Peter Novello. I was abducted as a child while my family was on holiday in Sicily–'

'Ah. I have a vague memory of the case.'

'Really? I'm surprised. It never played big in either country. Anyway, I was subsequently adopted by a couple in Glasgow called Philipson, and I became Christopher or Kit Philipson. My dad was German-born, and got out of the country just before the war.'

'One of the Jewish children?'

'Yes. His father was a man called Greenspan. Probably a pretty disreputable individual, possibly eventually fairly high up in the Mafia or Camorra in Sicily or Naples. It may be that he called himself Durataverdi.'

'Ah! Greenspan... You know, I never found Durataverdi a very convincing name, and I never found anybody else with the same name, though of course, families are an important factor in the Mafia's membership.'

'So you know of him?'

'Yes, I do. Or did.'

'Did? He's dead, then?'

'Possibly, but not so far as I know. He would be very old if he is still alive.'

'Why did you put him in the past tense, then?'

'Because the Mafia is a thing of the past for me. The idea of keeping up with it so I could bring the book up to date every ten years or so was repulsive to me. I wanted to wash my hands of them – wash the smell off. I'm now studying the later members of the Medici family.'

'Same difference.'

The scholar took over. 'Well, some points of resemblance, certainly.'

'It's a pity it's been so long since the publication of the book, but you still might have some information of interest to me.'

'Quite likely. I'm called on often by people who are engaged on the new and up-to-date definitive study of the Mafia. It seems like an obligation: if I give up on the subject, I ought to help my successors in the field.'

'I would be very grateful if you could add me to the list of those you could help. I'm not writing a book – would it be possible to get all the information you have on Durata-verdi?'

'Yes, no problem. But you're assuming I have a lot.'

'Well, I hoped–'

'And I do have a lot in quantity. It's the quality of it that's suspect. There's very little of substance there. Details of court appearances, conjectures about crimes he was involved in, some conjectures about his past – it all amounts to what has been called "a bucket of warm spit".'

'The American vice-presidency. And I don't think the man said "spit".'

'Right. But this man – your man – has been a figure of genuine importance in a widely publicised organisation, and yet he leaves behind almost nothing. He must have been, or be, a man with a marvellous capacity for covering his tracks. And of course, he was brilliant at getting himself accepted by the Mafia in the first place. He had a unique ability to reinvent himself. I have just scraps about him where there should be meaty chunks. Do you get me?'

'I think so. You're saying you're not what I need.'

'Yes. I haven't got what you need.'

'But someone else has?'

'Yes. He knows everything there is to know about the Mafia. He can't use it. Quite apart from legal actions, libel and so on, there is the possibility that they'd cut the cackle and have him killed. In fact, I'd say there's a certainty of that. So he has all the stories – some well authenticated, some the sort of story that goes round in criminal organisations and gets blown up, exaggerated.'

'I can guess. But would he be willing to help me?'

'He might be. In confidence I can tell you

that there is probably a degree of collusion and collaboration between him and the Mafia high-ups. If he has something the Mafia wants to know about, then things might be arranged, maybe a meeting.'

'And the thing the Mafia might want to know about?'

'It's possible it might be you. The Mafia, as I say, is hot on family.'

'I don't get the impression that Walter Greenspan is, or was, hot on family.'

'That may have changed with age. It often does. Alternatively he may feel bound to pretend to some family pride to fit in with the pattern of the organisation he now belongs to.'

'Alternatively he may be dead.'

'Oh yes, certainly. What you do in that case I don't know. Talk to Pietro, I suppose. That's Pietro Conti, the man I'm referring to. He uses my archives, by the way, so I'll only be calling in several favours. I'm sure he'll try to help, but whether he can or not depends on the Mafia, or simply on Greenspan perhaps.'

'I'll cross my fingers.'

'Look, your seven minutes is well up. I'll send you all I have and I'll include Conti's Palermo address and other details. I'll email him in advance, so you have some kind of introduction. I'm off – I've got a seminar now. Good luck.'

I'll need it, thought Kit.

The material when it arrived was as slight as Marston had suggested it would be. Kit picked up the date of the trial at which Greenspan had become, in a limited way, a public figure, and there were one or two meagre items of information – a birth date (1916 – surely untrue, a number plucked from the air like an actress's birth date), a school in Vienna, a graduation date from the university of Frankfurt. Kit decided to keep an open mind about all the information he got about Greenspan from an Italian source. He himself calculated a birth date from the background information he had. Hilde Greenspan (so called) was eight when she took the Kindertransport train to London. Her birthdate, then, was circa 1931. It was unlikely that her father was less than twenty when she was born, and he was probably older, so he would be approaching his centenary if he was alive. Perfectly possible. Lots of people became centenarians. The last British man alive to have fought in the First World War trenches had just died, aged 113.

Then he thought again. Greenspan could have become a father at seventeen – or fifteen come to that. Plenty of people, male and female, did that today. The Weimar Republic was a hotbed of sexual varieties, each mingling and mixing, each with its own bars and clubs where like could meet like. Walter Greenspan could have been born in 1914. He could even have been born in 1916 as he had claimed. Kit tore up the paper with his mathematical calculations.

His adoptive grandfather was very old. Kit needed no more than that.

He could, obviously, be senile. He could have delusions, and they could very likely be delusions about his past. He could be passing through life barely conscious of what was going on around him. Kit had, so far, no grounds for optimism, except for the fact that nobody apparently had hard evidence of his death.

He left it five days before he rang Pietro Conti. He preferred the telephone to email, and to the inadequacies of the Italian postal service.

Pietro Conti was openness itself. He had been contacted by Marston, he had started making tentative enquiries, but the Mafia had its own bureaucracy just as legally established political governments did. Could Kit hold himself ready? Yes, he could.

'And could you be prepared to put yourself entirely into my hands – or rather not my hands but the hands of the person nominated by the Mafia hierarchy?'

'Yes, entirely. I'll wait for your call.'

Kit waited for six days, keeping his mobile at the ready.

'Mr Philipson?'

At last it had come. The voice was Pietro's, heavily accented but not difficult to understand.

'Can you put down everything and come?'

'It's what I want more than anything.'

'Get a flight to Palermo. I've booked you a room in the Hotel Lampedusa. You will be collected either from there or from my flat here. You will be taken to a car, blindfolded, then driven to a location where you will meet Durataverdi as he is always called here, and will be allowed to talk to him. That can be as long as you like for the one day, but he is very old, and must be allowed breaks if he asks for them.'

'Of course. I'm not a slave-driver. Anyway I'm in their power.'

'*È vero – totalmente*. I'll speak to you when you arrive at the hotel.'

'I can ring you – I don't know when I'll arrive.'

'I will be told when you arrive.'

Kit threw a change of clothes into a small suitcase, went straight to the airport, then booked an evening flight to Heathrow, and an early morning one next day to Palermo. He had been often to Heathrow with his parents, and he found it was even worse without them – more lonely, more hostile, more faceless. His overnight hotel had pretty much the same profile. It was a relief to get to Palermo, but he stuck to his hotel room, where quite soon a phone call came through from Pietro Conti: tomorrow at nine he would be fetched. He'd better get the best breakfast he could in the hotel, and maybe take a few snacks, because the Mafia did not see themselves as purveyors of fast food to curious outsiders. Kit spent the rest of the day walking around Palermo, acquiring in the process bars of chocolate and packets of nuts.

There was a knock on his hotel door almost exactly at nine o'clock next morning. When he opened it he saw a man of the utmost insignificance: short and skinny, with a blob for a face. Rather a disappointment, he told himself with a wry smile. Even a mother would find it difficult to love a face like that. The local Mafia, he conjectured, was telling him he had a very low place in their hierarchy of importance. He nodded, shook hands, then let himself be taken to the car.

He was pushed into the front seat, and as his driver went round the front of the car he felt a blindfold being put round his head from behind. He had an escort of two, then. The blindfold was tied most expertly, then his hands were cuffed in front of him. Nobody worried that the street was crowded with people, almost all of whom could see what was going on. The driver put the car into gear and drove off.

'We do not talk,' the unappetising driver said.

That was that, then. Darkness, and silence.

Kit did not try to keep a mental record of the turns, reverses and variations of speed. He was being taken to somewhere that he was not expected to identify. There was precious little he could do about that, and he did not want to do anything. Identifying where his grandfather now lived out his last years was the least of his imperatives. He presumed the Mafia was afraid of a further charge being made against him. He himself felt that Walter Greenspan was of an age that should put him beyond charges. All he wanted was to be told the truth about the past. Was Greenspan capable of the truth?

Gradually the artificial blackout of the blindfold began to get to him. He was without the gift of sight, and he was totally at the mercy of these two individuals, the presumed servants of a worldwide crime conspiracy. He began to feel the blood rush to his face, to feel the sweat soaking his shirt in the small of his back. He wanted to yell out, to show himself he existed, and could act independently. He began to contemplate opening his mouth and calling out his name.

'We are here,' said the voice in heavily accented English. Kit estimated that they had been driving about forty or forty-five minutes.

He let himself be taken from the car. He was led a few steps forward, then a door was opened and he was taken through it. There was a fumbling at the back of his head, and suddenly the world was light again. But he was hurried up a staircase in what he reckoned to be a fairly large rural dwelling, furnished and decorated basically, for occasional use. Not, then, his grandfather's home, but a place he had been brought to. This was confirmed when he was led into a large room, with much more light, but very little furniture. He thought this must be the bedroom floor, with the two rooms put together.

In the centre of the room there was a high-backed upright chair all on its own. No table, no glass of water – not for the interviewer, nor for the interviewee – no mod cons. The man seated needed nothing, the meeting seemed designed to suggest.

Kit gestured to the floor and said: 'Chair.' His feeble companion shrugged and went to fetch one from downstairs. While he was gone Kit could take in the other figure in the room.

He sat in the imposing chair, his forearms stretched along the arms, clutching a wooden knob on the end of each. He was not small, but he gave the impression of having become shrivelled by his great age. Perhaps his shiny suit had fitted him last year, or the year before that, but it had become baggy as time continued to roll over the old man's head. The man's body had at some time been impressive, Kit guessed, but the shoulders seemed to have drooped, the legs contracted, so that it could almost have been a doll sitting there. Kit was looking at the ashes of an impressive and imposing man who was a law unto himself.

But it was the face that intrigued him most. The eyes were alive, as the rest of the man hardly was. They blazed, burning but not warming the observer. Kit was reminded of Frank Novello, whose eyes and mouth announced that conscience and truth were things that had never had any relevance for him, held no meaning for him. But with this man the eyes seemed like something manufactured, whereas the mouth showed directly contradictory indications: at one moment twisted with a grimace of contempt, at others shifting to a sort of uncertainty – an instinct to be merciful, helpful, companionable. And it was an expression that was almost immediately wiped off and replaced again by the grimaces.

How does one survive in a world gone mad, Kit asked himself? And not just mad, but bad too – a world in which all the advances made over the centuries in compassion, understanding and fellow feeling were thrown aside and replaced by emotions and principles which were atavistic, savage, medieval – or rather from the Dark Ages.

The face was now decked out with the old man's dominant emotion: this boy will never be anything in my worlds – the worlds I've inhabited during my lifetime.

The man from the back seat of the car now came into the room and went and stood by the large chair. He was carrying a big book that looked like a Bible. Kit was glad of his chair, felt it was a concession, but he knew that if he asked for a pen and paper they would not have been given him.

'Who are you?' the old man in the chair croaked. His English was workmanlike, and the translator beside him was largely irrelevant, probably acting as a spy. Suddenly Kit realised that the book he was holding must be a dictionary.

'I am Christopher Philipson. I am the adoptive son of Jürgen Philipson, who I believe was your son by Elisabeth Greenspan.'

The blazing eyes blinked, then eyebrows were raised. The voice remained harsh.

'There was no such person. Whether the woman who called herself such was the mother of my children or anybody's else's children, I never enquired. What point was there in disputing it? They would never get money from me except by my wish and on my terms. There were many claims from women, but very little money changed hands.'

The translator seemed to nervously condense the words before he began to repeat them to Kit, but Durataverdi silenced him with a wave of the hand. He needed no translator.

'But you did have connections,' insisted Kit. 'Money was provided when Elisabeth's children were sent to England.'

The hand waved again dismissively.

'Loose change,' the old man said. Kit felt there was starting to be a barrier between them.

'Could we start again?' he asked. There was the briefest of nods. 'Who are you? What was your background? What were you doing when my father and Aunt Hilda were born?'

The man's mouth softened again as memory started moving.

'My father was an official in the Austrian Imperial Civil Service. He was prosperous under the emperor, much less prosperous after the First War, under the Republic. He and my mother, who was a Catholic, scrimped and saved to send me to university, but when I was fifteen I told them that that was the last thing I wanted. I packed my bags and got out. I never saw them again.'

'How did you live?'

'I saw how things were going with the Nazi

Party in Germany. I sold the Jews protection. Good protection at a fair price.'

'But the time came when protection was not much use.'

'It was not possible,' he was corrected. 'It was a totally new world. What was moral and legal on Wednesday was immoral and illegal on Thursday. One had to be a gadfly merely to keep up. I acted as travel agent for the smarter Jews who realised this early on. I got them out of Germany and I got their money out as well, or as much of it as I could. It was dangerous, but it was also lucrative. I enjoyed myself.'

'You had a good time with women?'

'I have always. Always there were women. Men too. You have talked to Herr Erheim in Vienna, have you not? I hear things. There are no secrets. I met him first in a homosexual bar. He was a young boy too green to know what it was. There were lots of English went there, and that should have told him. He became one of my best assistants. Today he is a national hero, which I find very funny.'

'And where did you meet the woman who called herself Elisabeth Greenspan?' said Kit, unwilling to let her go.

'What she called herself is irrelevant. There were many Greenspans – at that time. If she had claimed to be my wife she'd soon have learnt what sort of wedding ceremony it was that she'd gone through... Where did I meet her, you ask? I can't remember. Does it matter? They tell me hardly anyone gets married these days, even in Italy... In the way of business I went to lots of synagogues. Praise the Lord and make good contacts. Her father was a rabbi.'

'And you and Erheim ran a sort of travel agency for Jews?'

'I ran it. Erheim was my junior. Very junior.'

'But in the early 1940s you were forced to leave Austria and Germany?'

'It was getting too hot for me to stay. My German contact was getting scared, and wanted to end it all. Without his co-operation it was pointless to stay.'

'But why come to Italy?'

Durataverdi almost assumed the stance of a teacher, even wagging his fingers.

'Crossing over to an Allied or a neutral country was very difficult. And nobody thought at that time the Allied countries would win. Being a neutral country was no shield against Nazi aggression. Look at Norway, and Belgium. I came to Italy because Mussolini was indifferent on racial matters – and in any case I don't look Jewish. I was, in fact, half and half, and my appearance was often a splendid protection. Half the people who died in the chambers did so because they looked Jewish. My mother, as

I said, was Catholic, which helped after the peace in Italy. I would fit in more easily.'

'So you came to Italy, and that was the easy bit. What did you do after you settled here?'

'Travelled around making contacts.'

'The same sort of business as you were used to?'

'Some of that, but at that point people weren't so keen to get out of Italy. Tip a few thousand lire to the right person and life was good. No, most of my work involved making contact with the various Italian criminal fraternities. I enjoyed that. I learnt Italian pretty quickly, and claimed to be the son of an Italian restaurateur in Innsbruck. I made a good Italian, I'm their type. Things were looking good – they were good.'

'But you were imprisoned in Ferramonti.'

The old figure in the chair shrugged his shoulders, shrivelled and near powerless. But more powerful was the force of his wicked smile.

'A mere hiccup. A blip you say today, do you not?' He looked up at the translator, who spread out his hands in bewilderment.

'Blip is the word,' said Kit.

'I was imprisoned as a member of the Mafia. Nothing was going to happen to me. The Jewish prisoners were in a majority, and all of them were in danger, but I was not. I made more contacts in jail than I ever made out of jail. That's what I'd come to the south of Italy to do, after all.'

'And did you intend to defect to the Allies?'

'I thought of it. That was quite a difficult matter. The British and American troops had landed in Sicily, but when they got to the mainland the fighting was indecisive. Things went this way and that, and it was not easy to decide what to do.'

'You mean whether to defect to the Allied side or not?'

'Basically so. Making the wrong decision could prove fatal. You don't think I'm silly enough to defect to the losing side, do you? For reasons of conscience? A thousand noes! If the Allied troops were chased out of Italy they wouldn't be taking any defectors with them. I waited, temporised, until the picture sorted itself out.'

'But eventually you defected to the Allied side?'

'Yes.'

'Because they looked like the winning side?'

'Of course.'

Kit had wondered whether he could get from his grandfather some trace of conscience or scruple, anything that spoke of a moral choice having been made. So far there was very little trace of one. It was as if his own wellbeing was the only good he recognised.

'I think we can jump forward,' Kit said. 'I don't want to tire you.'

'You won't tire me,' the old man said. 'It doesn't look as if you are likely to interest me much either.'

'It all interests me,' said Kit with an academic's sharpness. 'It's all new to me even if it's old hat to you. I suppose you could say you found your spiritual home in the Mafia.'

'Spirit? Bah! None of that nonsense.'

'Your natural home, then.'

'That's better.'

'You were recognised as a man of a thousand talents, you were accepted, and you became a wheeler-dealer as we call it. *"Figaro qua, Figaro là."* You need it done, we can do it for you.'

'Now you're not doing so bad for an English boy.'

'And I suppose you made your way up the hierarchy?'

'That's right, but never in the way that some hierarchies work – you rise up in the organisation and you stop doing any of the basic things, the things that you're good at and those that made you noticed. That's never been my way, or the Mafia way. That's why the ridiculous Italian police caught me and put me on trial: I was still getting my hands dirty.'

'I understand. In Britain if you're a good

283

teacher they make you into a headmaster, where you don't teach at all.'

Greenspan smiled a cynical smile.

'That's probably so you don't show up the mediocre teachers, who are the vast majority. Schools – how boring they usually are! I went to life, my best teacher, and it didn't fail me.'

'Did life ever take you to Britain?'

A quick glance shot out in Kit's direction.

'I suppose you know it did.'

'I know nothing at all. I guessed you were there.'

'You guessed right. The visit you are interested in was probably one made in the spring of 1990.'

'When I was nearly three.'

'That's right. And my visit was to Glasgow. I call it a visit but it was not a holiday or a sightseeing trip. Which was lucky because it rained all the time I was there.'

'Glasgow is not a sunny place,' said Kit.

'It made a change after Naples,' Greenspan said, almost courteously.

'I presume your visit had something to do with the gang wars.'

'Exactly. And why should someone who knows the Mafia through and through be called in? Because the Mafia runs all through the ice cream wars and all the other ones. And when we talk about "the Mafia' we have to remember that we are talking not about one organisation, a monolith, but about a hundred organisations, little ones sheltered under an umbrella, usually originating from one of the many small villages in Calabria or Sicily. When you understand that you are dealing with a jigsaw of small pieces, you are taking the first steps on the way to understanding the problems and being able to solve them.'

Kit nodded. Already he was feeling more relaxed, because he felt the old rascal was beginning to trust him.

'Tell me about this memorable visit to Glasgow.'

Greenspan shifted in his seat, and a wicked expression played on his face.

'It was a sort of peace conference – like Yalta in 1945 – if not peace, then plotting the dimensions of the Cold War. I was there to keep the real negotiators informed. I sat in on some of the sessions but I seldom spoke. What I often did was talk to the delegates, filling them in on the background, which gave body and history to what seemed like utterly trivial disputes. And, of course, sometimes we just talked.'

Kit leant forward in his chair.

'And of course, you often "just talked" with my father, or my so-called father.'

'You're talking about Mr Novello?'

'That's right.'

'I think he was your father. He more or less admitted it was possible – and if he was prepared to admit that why would anybody else bother themselves with it?'

'He denied being my father when I visited him in the nursing home where he now lives. I wondered whether he was getting himself into the sort of muddle about people that Alzheimer's sufferers often get into.'

'Very likely. Thank God – who does not exist – I've never shown any signs of Alzheimer's or other senile afflictions. Let me tell you why I feel confident that Francesco – Frank you call him? – is your father.'

'Please do. I'd like to have it clear, and I'd like to know the nature of his marriage.'

'Oh, I believe that on the surface it was fine, a model marriage. They were both of one mind: she was devoted to him, and he was devoted to him too. So it was a loving, fruitful marriage and he had five or six regular women friends whom he could go to when the fancy took him. Some of them, who were changed regularly, were women he had helped in his job – getting them out of legal fixes and so on.'

'He told you all this?'

'Yes, he told me. Over a drink, over meals. I urged him to talk. I like to know about my possible adversaries.'

'Did you and he click at once?'

'At once. Across a crowded room, you might say. The click came because I know the type so well. He told me about the six ladies

286

because he knew I'd already guessed. And I knew he knew I'd already guessed. So I could lead the conversation on to the next stage of marriages that seemed to be made in heaven.'

'The breakdown of those marriages?'

'Of course.' He leered. 'How could such a marriage continue for long? Neither men nor women are naturally monogamous. First of all things go well, and they did for Frank and his wife. They had a girl and a boy, the ideal of a natural marriage, marriage as photographed by a society photographer. And then there is a little disagreement. She wants more children. He does not. Children cost too much in the way of time and attention. She thinks children are the whole meaning of life. She is a Catholic in this, though in other ways her Catholicism is skin-deep. She gets pregnant, and Frank suspects this is because she has left off taking the pill. When you arrive in the world Frank sees only his wife in your face, her in your walk, her in toto. Then he gets taken over by even more extreme ideas.'

'He thinks I am the son of some actor called Harry Bradley-Perle.'

'Ah, you discovered that. So he told me. It justified Novello in taking no notice of you.'

An idea struck Kit.

'Did Isla think: if he's going to clutch on to a silly illusion like that I might as well make it a reality?'

'Something like that. You realise I kept

myself informed of his affairs through my Glasgow contacts.'

'Why do that?'

'Because you could never know when they might come in useful. All my whole life – my career, let's call it – was based on storing knowledge. And there was a special reason for doing it too.'

'What was that?'

'When I met Frank he was a third-time father. You were about three years old. The poison had been working in his mind all those three years. He told me all about you and he obviously wanted to believe that this minor actor was your father. And at one point he said, "It would serve her right if I got someone to abduct the little bastard."'

'And you looked at each other...'

Greenspan looked ridiculously pleased.

'Exactly! I misjudged you. You're quite a sharp boy. We looked at each other and he put me down for possible future use and I put him down for possible future use.'

'You can't have needed money by then?'

'Now you are being silly. One always needs money. Money's power. There was another reason why I kept myself well informed about Frank.'

'What was that?'

'I had a particular use for an abducted child.'

'You'd been in touch with Jürgen?'

'Yes. One of those fantastic coincidences that turn out to be a little more – or perhaps I mean a little less – than a coincidence. I met him on the last day of that conference – the one we've been talking about.'

'But that must have been a coincidence, surely?'

'Not entirely, in fact. Jürgen had been in touch with me. He was one of many who'd been in touch with Helmut Erheim in Vienna after the war, and he'd heard of the name Durataverdi. When the Italian government started its big anti-Mafia crusade the name cropped up in English newspapers, and Jürgen used the consulate in Naples to get the address of my lawyer. He sent me, through the lawyer, a letter – a long letter telling me about his loss of his mother, his happiness with the Philipsons, his sister, his work, his marriage to an art expert who was quite often in Italy. He wondered if I thought it a good idea that we got in touch.'

'And you said yes?' said Kit, surprised.

'I said no! Silly boy – what use could he be to me? But then when the Glasgow peacemakings came up, it amused me to go, and I wondered if I should just contact him, talk to him about my great achievements as a Mafia capo. It would amuse me. I had met my daughter in Vienna. She had wanted to like me, but had failed. I tried to woo her, so to speak, but she had found me unattractive, uncharming. She thought us Machiavellian. Apparently she never told her brother about the visit.' He shrugged. 'In the event Jürgen turned up on the last day, when peace was secure – for a time at any rate – and I was introduced to the deputy editor of the *Glasgow Examiner.*'

'He realised who you were?'

'Oh yes, of course. We talked – calmly, sensibly – which came naturally to Jürgen, and I could put on a good performance when needed. I told him I had replied negatively to his letter because I didn't think someone who had been involved for years with the Mafia and the Camorra would be a good father for a crusading journalist to have. We circled round all sorts of subjects until eventually I said: "No children yet?" And I could tell by the look of pain how deeply that fact hurt him. I made a sudden decision. I said: "I know someone – a sister of my current woman – who's had an illegitimate baby, which she kept, and she bitterly regrets that decision. She hasn't made a second decision about it yet – it's a big one for an Italian woman – but if she does...?" and he said at once: "I am interested." I said: "The child is half English," and he said: "It couldn't matter less." I said: "This sort of arrangement, quite informal, is common in Italy. If any decision is made I'll let you know." And so the deal was made.'

There was silence in the bare room as Kit digested this.

'I think I can understand my father's succumbing to the offer. There was no question of abduction, and there was apparently a genuine and close connection with the donor. But why on earth did you make the offer to him? What was in it for you?'

'Power. It amused me to have a son who was part of the liberal, high-thinking class, albeit in a little, powerless country like Scotland. I knew that if he took the child he would be in my power. I would be magnanimous, I would not involve him in any of the sordid and bloody little crimes I was often party to. But I also knew he was mine.'

'But you never used that power.'

'No, I never used it,' said Greenspan, almost as if he was ashamed. 'Perhaps I liked him too much. Perhaps he was just too good for me to get pleasure from manipulating him, forcing him to stain that purity he had. I had always got pleasure from power, but I enjoyed exercising it on those who were twisted creatures like me, people who would gladly stoop to anything. I proved myself of the same kind as them, but cleverer, more ruthless, more inhuman and inhumane. That I got great pleasure from. But a good man, one who never stooped, one who examined every step he made morally – I thought about it, and concluded it would not suit me.'

'I see,' said Kit. 'Jürgen sometimes had the effect of making people better than they seemed.'

'I think Hilde had something of that quality too. As I told you, I met her once in Vienna, but I put her off me – I could not pretend to her. Where her quality – their quality – came from I don't know.'

'Their mother?' put in Kit softly.

'Maybe, maybe,' said Greenspan, surprisingly. 'Maybe I stayed my hand in Jürgen's case because the watch on me by the Italian state was by then too close for comfort. And the nearer you came to coming of age the less power I had.'

'Did you know he was told I was abducted?'

The old man perked up immediately.

'No. Who told him? It must have been Frank.'

'Yes, it was Frank.'

'And why did he do it? Power, like me?'

'Not exactly. He did it six or seven years ago. I think he was in the early stages of Alzheimer's. It may have been some sort of revenge. Frank may have thought my father got on his high moral horse too readily. Who can say what thought processes are going through the mind of an Alzheimer's sufferer?'

'True,' said Greenspan, with some kind of relish in his voice. Then he sank for a moment into thought. 'You know,' he said at last, 'you were really very lucky.'

'Lucky? To be abducted?'

'Yes. You had an ideal childhood, in the care of people who were loving and very conscientious. You may have felt stifled by their goodness, but you were safe.'

'Perhaps... Yes, looking back it feels like a very good childhood. Perhaps a lot better than I would have had with the Novellos, in spite of Isla's love and care.'

The old man again had a look of relish in his eyes as he asked: 'Have you ever wondered whether she was party to the abduction?'

'Not until now. Everybody has always said she was devoted to me.'

'Everyone seems to have been devoted to you. She was also, people say, devoted to Frank, at least in the early stages of the marriage. Were her devotions altogether a good thing, do you think?'

'In what way?'

'Your great philosopher Oscar Wilde – what was it he said? She loved him "with a love that made his life a burden". He tests that love to the absolute limit, and still she says "yes" and remains devoted. What is he to do? All he can do is throw her away. All she can do is hold out for the biggest pay she can get.'

'You don't know this,' said Kit.

'I read it in his eyes, his squirms, his anger

293

every time I talked to him in Glasgow. What happened after the abduction makes me convinced I was right. She remained quiet. And why should you complain?'

'I don't understand what you mean.'

'You had a good childhood. Will your adulthood conceivably live up to it? Adult challenges are much more difficult to survive than childish ones.'

'Many people would say the opposite was closer to the truth.'

'Would they? I had a nasty, restrictive childhood. My parents wanted to push me into the civil service, make me a government stooge like themselves. Imagine what harm I could have done in that kind of job after the government of Germany took control of Austria. Instead I made my own way, my own career, my own lifestyle. And my own moral code. Remember, I did a great deal of good as well as some harm. The good always included a sweetener for me – of course it did. How else could I have lived, enjoyed a few of the good things of life? But good came out of it to the people who used me as well.'

'You're not on trial in my mind,' said Kit.

'Maybe not. But I don't think you have any idea of what living in a murderous dictatorship is like. All moral guidelines have been thrown out the window. You have to live each day as though it's your last. You have to make your own moral code, yes, but you also have to be ready to tear it up if following it is going to endanger your life.'

'Morally you were an improviser,' suggested Kit.

'I had to be. Also I rather enjoyed it. I was one of those smart boys who enjoy a gamble, enjoy using people because it enlarges their understanding of human types, enjoy being in control.'

'Nobody could doubt that,' said Kit. 'But couldn't you have used your talents with more kindness and mercy? I'm thinking of my grandmother.'

Greenspan gave his usual shrug.

'Maybe I could. I did not try. You can't imagine the wicked pleasure of having a woman entirely at my beck and call – a good woman, too, though not very bright, to put it mildly. She loved me after every first night we had together – because this was an occasional relationship, you understand, a matter of visits now and then. I would have got her out of Germany if I could have, just so I could wash my hands of her for ever. No such luck. But I never went to her after she saw her children off to London. War broke out, every difficult thing became ten times more difficult; my skills were tested every day of my life and before long I began planning for Italy, and a new life there.'

'Where you became involved with the Mafia.'

'Inevitably. You could say they were waiting for me.'

'And eventually you planned an abduction, to provide your son, her son, with a child.'

'I did. That was in 1990. I did it gladly, had a well-oiled machine, and everything went according to plan.'

'Yes, it did. I never suspected I was being abducted.'

Greenspan laughed.

'You were only three. A few years more and you would have understood. You are a bright boy, like I said. Is that all? Can I return to my life on the edge of the law?'

'I suppose so,' said Kit, after a moment's thought.

'You are sure there is nothing more you want to ask me? Ask now because there will be no second opportunity.'

There was silence in the room.

'Did Frank openly ask you to abduct me, his child?'

Greenspan shook his head at Kit's naivety;

'Openly? What is openly? After I had met Jürgen I met again with Frank. He spoke to me about his doubts about your paternity, the impossibility of his accepting you, the mistrust of his wife that was always in his mind. He looked at me. I looked at him. Then we got down to planning it.'

Kit thought.

'That was real wickedness,' he said.

'Apparently he cared nothing about who I was given to, whether I would live or die – cared about nothing but himself.'

'Yes, you're right. You're seeing that there is greater wickedness than mine. And remember that Frank had always lived in safe, fair old England, under the rule of law. He had never known the sort of place where yesterday's acceptable behaviour becomes tomorrow's capital offence. He had never known the madness of the modern state that embraces the extreme and the insane and makes them the norm. I reacted to my circumstances in my way, but I was not born evil. I just chose it as the only way I could survive. Good morning, Mr Philipson.'

Kit waited to say something, but he didn't know what. A man entered the room and he felt a touch on his arm. He was cuffed and blindfolded and led out to the car.

On the way back to Palermo he wondered about the new angle he had acquired on Isla. Was she victim or collaborator? Had she chosen Frank over her three-year-old child? Was it her knowledge of Frank's part in the abduction that enabled her to gain a lavish settlement when the divorce was finalised?

And did he care now?

In the plane from Palermo to Heathrow Kit meditated on the three mothers whose lives and values had figured so largely in his own and his father's lives. In the centre,

Genevieve, loving, self-sacrificing, warm. On one side of her, Elisabeth, whom many of the actors in the story thought of as stupid beyond measuring. Could not she be seen as a kind of holy fool, always sacrificing herself for others, up to the final hideous sacrifice of her own beloved children? And on the other side was Isla – the sort of mother, Kit now saw, who was so preoccupied with her own wishes and needs that she could be seen as conniving in her own child's abduction in a final desperate attempt to hold on to her husband's love. Perhaps there was no villainy in this story, but if there was, it was surely Isla. Kit let his thoughts stray to the man he had just met for the first and last time. He was cunning, ruthless, mendacious – all sorts of undeniable qualities at his command when necessary, and in more terrifying forms than the softer versions shown by men and women in liberal, democratic regimes.

When it came to judging, Kit felt he had to ask himself: what would you have done if you had lived in a world gone mad? Greenspan had cut himself off from family, class and religion, and no sooner had he done so than the world of Central Europe had gone crazy. The more Kit learnt about the decade from the mid-Thirties to the end of the war, the more he saw it as the product of demented sadists. If your world had been taken over by mass killers, torturers, slave-drivers, what could you do? Hide? Escape? Accept?

There was something about Greenspan's career in Fascist Europe that was ... not glorious, no, but that showed energy; a refusal to capitulate, a determination to win through, survive the general butchery. It was, in fact, the survival instinct seen in its most energetic, if least commendable, form.

Kit had bought an English newspaper at the bookstall in the airport. Death of Edward Upward at the age of 105. Friend of Auden and Isherwood, and lifelong member of the Communist party... So, a contemporary of his grandfather. A man who had lived in a stable, slightly sleepy democracy; and devoted his life to being an apologist for a murderous political extremism. Which would Kit prefer as a member of his family: the apologist for mass slaughter, or the jaunty, inventive, unscrupulous survivor, the man who was never going to be done down, never going to submit?

The latter, of course.

When he changed planes at Heathrow and caught the plane to Manchester he asked himself: what am I going to do? Here he was in possession of a house in a starchy area, a modest fortune in safe investments, a life ahead of him that could be conventional – research scholarships, academic jobs, even going into politics on a Lib Dem ticket? Would he insert the Novello family into the place in his life that had previously been filled by the Philipsons?

No, he would not. What was he to them? A stranger in the family, an intrusion, a none-too-welcome surprise. Was he any more than that even to Isla? Had she initially welcomed him as she did because she loved him as a mother, or because that was the reaction that he and other people would expect? Or because of her guilt at being a party to his abduction? No doubt in the future he would pay her occasional visits, which he certainly would not do to his father. Otherwise the Novellos had their world, their interests, and he had his.

What were those interests? That was what he had to find out. 'The world is all before you' – Genevieve had adapted Milton's phrase and applied it to him only days before she died. What would that world consist of? The answer would be for him to find and live up to. He thought that he would in the end try to make of himself something that the Philipsons would have recognised, something that they would have approved of.

When the plane landed at Manchester he turned away from the overhead corridor that would take him to the railway and to Leeds and went to buy himself a ticket on the next plane to Glasgow. The world was all before him indeed. An interlude in his life was over.

The publishers hope that this book has given you enjoyable reading. Large Print Books are especially designed to be as easy to see and hold as possible. If you wish a complete list of our books please ask at your local library or write directly to:

Magna Large Print Books
Magna House, Long Preston,
Skipton, North Yorkshire.
BD23 4ND